FOR THE LOVE OF BETTE

Fairfield Corners Book 4

L.A. REMENICKY

Lavish
Publishing LLC

First Edition

For the Love of Bette – Fairfield Corners Book Four

2022 Lavish Publishing, LLC

All Rights Reserved

Published in the United States by Lavish Publishing, LLC, Midland, Texas

Cover Design by: Victor R. Sosa

Cover Images: Canstock

Paperback edition

ISBN: 978-1-64900-050-7

www.LavishPublishing.com

Contents

Chapter One

WITH A YAWN, Dr. Mark Fairfield poured coffee out of the pot on the warmer as he reached for a lid, wondering why the back of his neck tingled as if someone was watching him. "Get a grip, Fairfield. It's just your imagination," he muttered to himself. He'd just worked a double at the hospital in Fort Wayne, so he made an unanticipated stop at the gas station just over the county line. Hoping the jolt of caffeine would keep him awake for the twenty-minute drive to his home on the other side of Fairfield Corners, he shuffled over toward the cashier. At two in the morning, he was surprised to spot another customer inside the store. The man hovered near the door as if waiting for someone. Mark couldn't tell if it was his imagination or if the guy was giving off the weird vibes. The man had his hands jammed in his coat pockets and a baseball cap pulled low over his eyes.

After paying for his coffee and a quick conversation with the clerk, he returned to his car and resumed his journey home. Normally, he enjoyed the ride home after a long shift. It gave him time to decompress, but tonight something was different. Maybe his apprehension was from the caffeine or the weird vibe he got from that other patron.

Headlights shining in his rearview mirror temporarily blinded him before the offending vehicle rushed past him, a Fairfield Corners sheriff's car in pursuit with sirens blaring. Recognizing the truck from the gas station, he shook his head and wondered if that was what had been giving him the weird vibe. Maybe the guy had been waiting for him to leave so he could rob the place.

Horrified but unable to look away, he winced at the squeal of tires and watched as the truck, top-heavy from the camper top, tipped over and slid down the highway on its side. Pulling up behind the police cruiser, he put his car in park and grabbed his medical bag out of the back seat.

Rushing up to the wreck, he recognized the officer struggling to open the driver's side door. "James, what can I do to help?"

"I thought that was you we passed." He wrenched open the door and peered into the cab of the truck. He jumped back as the driver heaved himself out of the opening and kicked at him. Wrestling him into position to be handcuffed, James peered into the cab. "Hey, there's someone else in here. Mark, can you see about the passenger while I get this guy secured?"

"Sure." Mark pulled himself up onto the side of the truck. "Shit, it's just a kid." Gently lowering himself into the vehicle, he crouched next to the boy who stared up at him. "It's okay, I'm a doctor. Don't move." He began checking for injuries. "What's your name?"

"Dane," the boy replied, his voice wavering.

"Hi, Dane. I'm Dr. Mark. Does it hurt anywhere?"

"Is my dad okay?"

"Yeah, my friend James is taking care of him. I'm more worried about you." He ran his hands over the boy's arms and legs, checking for obvious fractures and bruising. "Does this hurt?"

"No."

"Good thing you were wearing your seatbelt. Let's get you out of here."

Mark heard another patrol car arrive as he pulled himself up and out of the truck before lying flat to pull the boy up and out of the vehicle. When he had Dane clear of the opening, he turned to find a pair of hands lifting the boy down to the ground.

"Is that everyone?" Deputy Logan Miller asked.

"I believe so. The boy seems to be okay, but he should be checked out at the hospital."

A fire truck and ambulance arrived as he hopped down to the ground, so the firemen and EMTs took control of the situation. Standing off to the side, he watched the paramedics check over the boy and his father, the older man trying to convince them to remove the handcuffs. He heard a faint thumping noise that seemed to be coming from the camper.

The firemen were working with a tow truck driver to right the vehicle so it could be hauled away. He heard the winch kick on and the creak of metal as it pulled at the truck. As it started to move the thumping increased. "Stop," he yelled. "I think there's someone in the back."

Shutting off the winch, the firemen moved to the back of the camper and used a crowbar to pop open the door. He crawled into the camper, shining a flashlight around the dark interior. "Doc, we've got another victim in here!"

Mark stepped up into the camper and found the fireman removing what looked like a gag from her mouth.

"Help me!" she screamed, her eyes wild with fear as she strained against the ropes tied around her wrists and ankles. The weird feeling he'd gotten while at the gas station returned, making him almost dizzy with its intensity. *What is it about this woman?*

"Shhh, it's okay. We're here to help. I'm a doctor."

With a sob, she relaxed against him as he worked to untie the knots. The rope holding her wrists finally gave way, allowing him to check her arms for injuries. Gentle pressure elicited a groan from the victim.

"What's your name?"

"Bette Anderson. Oh, shit, that hurts."

"Hi Bette, I'm Mark and I'm a doctor. Is it okay if I take a look at your arm?"

"Sure."

"Well, Bette, looks like your arm is broken just above the elbow. Does it hurt anywhere else?"

"All over, but that's the worst."

He looked back out the door, "I need a splint to immobilize this arm and a cervical collar."

One of the EMTs handed him the items he requested. "We have a backboard ready once you have her arm splinted."

"This will hurt," he advised before he slid the splint under her arm. "I'll be as careful as possible, but I will have to move it a bit. I don't want to give you anything for the pain until you've been fully evaluated at the hospital."

Gently, he straightened her arm, frowning when she screamed.

"There, all done. I'm sorry for causing you pain."

Once they had her on the backboard, they loaded her into the ambulance along with the boy. The man who'd been driving was safely ensconced in the sheriff's car to be taken in for questioning about the gas station robbery and the woman they'd found tied up in the camper.

His tiredness gone, Mark followed the ambulance to the hospital. For some reason he didn't want to let Bette out of his sight.

Chapter Two

IT WAS ALMOST six in the morning by the time Mark finally arrived home. He'd spent a couple of hours at the Fairfield County Hospital making sure Bette was treated and settled into a room. For some reason he felt responsible for her safety and well-being.

Setting the sack of food on the counter, he rubbed his hands over his face, almost too tired to bother eating the meal he'd bought on his way home. The lateness of the hour made his only choice the truck stop and it's usually greasy but tasty fare. Looking around the kitchen, he wondered if he would be visited by the ghost of the house. His great Grandfather, Marcus Fairfield, haunted the home he'd built after the Civil War.

Growing up, he'd heard stories about the ghost from other kids but he'd never seen it for himself until he moved into the old house, intent on restoring it to its former glory. He still owned the construction company his father had started, so there had been no problem getting the electrical, plumbing, and drywall done in the main rooms before he'd moved in. He planned to do the finish work himself, having spent every summer working for his dad. Finishing a room with paint and stain had always been his favorite job until he'd discovered medicine.

A plate in one hand and a beer in the other, he settled onto the couch and touched a button on the remote to turn on the television. Not finding anything worth watching, he signed into his streaming service and selected his favorite show about a motorcycle club.

Losing himself in the storyline, he ate mechanically, his attention on the television. As he watched, the program changed. The color faded to black and white, and the building morphed into a southern plantation. He watched the light shining from an upstairs room flicker, as if from a candle before going out.

Creeping past the house, he hurried toward the creek and their spot. He'd seen Lizzie in Atlanta earlier that day and had passed her a note that said 9 p.m. She would know where to meet him at that time. Her father was a staunch Southern plantation owner, and he'd forbidden his daughter to see the Yankee officer, but her attraction to him had them contriving ways for them to be alone together. They'd made the spot under the willow tree at the bend in the creek their clandestine meeting place.

Wiping his hands on his trousers, he paced from the tree to the creek and back again, anxious to see his Lizzie. What was taking her so long?

The scrape of a slipper on the path had him swallowing hard to quell his nervousness—it had been over a week since their last meeting, and he was nervous she'd changed her mind about running away with him.

He leaned against the tree trunk and waited, wanting to be sure it was her and not someone else before he made his presence known.

"Marcus?"

His heart beat faster, feeling like it wanted to beat right out of his chest. She came! She'd chosen him. Sad that he'd be taking her away from her home, he resolved to give her a better life. He planned to return to northern Indiana and reopen his father's stone quarry. It wasn't his ambitions that her father despised, it was his heritage and political leanings. He'd forbidden Lizzie to see him, going so far as to hire a companion for her to keep her away from him. They'd managed to arrange a place where they could meet privately more often, near the creek that ran beside her home.

Dropping the satchel in her hand, she ran toward him, her face showing her joy at seeing him.

Sweeping her into his arms, he kissed her, forgetting himself for a moment and letting his hands roam up her back.

Her hands on his arms, she pushed him away lightly. "I've missed you so."

She looked at him. Her blue eyes matched the blue of her dress, and her blonde hair streamed down her back, released from the confines of the snood she normally wore to keep it neat as befitted a Southern belle.

Bringing her hands up to his face, he kissed them. "I wasn't sure you would come. Giving up your home and family is a huge step."

Folding her hands primly, she looked down and mumbled, "I can't leave with you tonight. My father is having a dinner party tomorrow evening and I'll be missed if I'm not there. He's leaving for Mobile directly after dinner, so I will be able to leave once he's gone."

"For you, my love, I would wait an eternity. Meet me here tomorrow evening at the same time?"

"Yes, and I brought some of my things tonight, so it will be easier for me to sneak out tomorrow. It's just a few personal items that won't be missed." She frowned as she stepped closer to him. "I need to get back. Father is watching me closely after he caught me smiling at you at the ball last Saturday night."

He kissed her hand, holding it longer than was proper. "Until tomorrow night."

Reluctantly, she turned to the path and took a few steps before turning back to face him. "Goodnight, my love."

She spun around and raced away, her voluminous skirts swaying.

Tomorrow they'd embark on their life together, away from her domineering father. He hated the secrecy and the hiding, but he would do anything for his Lizzie.

The theme song from the show he'd been watching blared from the television speakers, pulling him from the dream. What a dream, it had felt so real. But who was this Lizzie? His great grandfather had been married to Mary Wilding. He didn't remember anyone ever mentioning a Lizzie. In fact, when Mary died giving birth to Marcus's son, Marcus had shut himself away in this house after sending the baby to town with the nanny. He'd lived alone, only leaving the house to tend to his business until his death. No one else had lived in the house full-time until he'd moved in a month ago.

He'd initially worried about the stories of Marcus's ghost haunting the house, but he brushed it off to being urban legend after the construction workers had no sightings of the ghost. Sure, Adam had seen something when he rescued Ragan from Mark's brother, Billy, but that was a special circumstance. He'd been seeing things out of the corner of his eye but nothing full-on or in his face. Maybe there was some truth to the stories.

"Marcus, was that dream about you?" he asked aloud, feeling silly talking to an empty house. When he received no response he snorted and muttered, "I knew it was just a bunch of stories." The stairs creaked as if someone was walking up from the ground floor. "Old houses settle, that's all it is."

Padding up the stairs in his bare feet, he turned off the hallway light, not noticing the figure blocking the moonlight from the window. "I'm going to bed now. I'd appreciate it if you'd keep the noise down." Feeling foolish, he readied himself for bed, crawling under the covers with a sigh. He'd been up for almost twenty-four hours and was beyond tired.

It was almost noon when the slamming of a door jolted him from a sound sleep. "What the hell?" With a glance at the clock, he groaned and lay back down. "The day's half over already. Guess I better get up and get moving if I want to check on Bette before my shift tonight." Too bad he was scheduled at the hospital in Fort Wayne. He was covering for a vacationing doctor and would go back to working at the county hospital the following week.

Soon, the kitchen was filled with the scent of coffee and bacon. He sipped at the strong brew in his mug as he turned the two lonely strips of bacon. Reaching over, he put his hand on the paper towel roll and realized it was empty. "Crap, I forgot to grab a new roll." After the stove had been turned off, he turned to go to the pantry and yelled when he noticed a figure standing in front of the pantry door. Even without a hat, Mark recognized the uniform of a Union soldier. Captain's bars on the shoulders and gold stripes down the dark blue trousers denoted an officer. "I recognize you, you're Marcus Fairfield. Why are you haunting this house? You've been dead for many years."

The apparition frowned and showed Mark a ring. Made of gold fili-gree, it was obviously for a woman. "Is this Mary's ring?"

Shaking his head, the ghost gripped the ring tightly in his hand. "Find her," he said before he faded away.

"Find who?"

Chapter Three

BETTE GRUMBLED at the bright light being shined in her left eye, and then her right. What was it about hospitals and not letting you sleep for more than an hour at a time?

She had hoped the whole getting kidnapped thing was a nightmare, but no such luck. The security guard had been busy when she locked up the store, so she had walked to her car alone, even though there had been a rash of attacks in the mall parking lot. When she felt the hands grab her arms, all she could think about was how stupid she'd been to walk out there alone that late at night. Her purse had dropped to the ground before she'd had time to pull out her pepper spray. The hands clamped down harder the more she struggled.

"You'll do just fine. I bet you'll be a good momma for my boy," he'd whispered in her ear as he'd opened the door on a truck camper. When she'd refused to step up into the truck, he'd physically picked her up and shoved her in. "You're going to learn to not disobey me. Now, sit down."

With no other options, she'd sat with tears rolling down her face as he tied her wrists and ankles before gagging her with a handkerchief. *Why me? What does he want? What did he mean when he said I'd be a good momma?*

The musty smell of the thin mattress beneath her made her head thump, so she closed her eyes and tried to sleep, praying someone would find her. With no sense of time, she had no idea how long or how far they'd gone. She shuddered at the memory of the stop they'd made where he'd untied her ankles and then dragged her off into the woods and stripped off her underwear. She'd been terrified he was about to rape her, but all he did was turn his back and tell her to relieve herself as she wouldn't get another chance for quite a while. Thankful she'd worn a skirt to work that day, she'd done as he demanded while holding her skirt out of the way. The stop had taken no more than ten minutes and no cars had passed them. Her hope for rescue dwindled with each minute that ticked by.

Clenching and unclenching her hands to try and keep the blood flowing, she prayed for rescue. She'd been asleep when the increased speed woke her as the camper swayed, she'd rolled onto the floor just before the world turned upside-down. When she'd landed on her arm against the edge of the bunk, the sickening crack and blinding pain had her swallowing hard to keep from vomiting. She knew throwing up while gagged would probably cause her to asphyxiate and die. When she heard sirens, she'd been terrified the man would panic and hurt her worse than the pain in her arm. She thought she heard the man yelling about letting him go, so she took a chance and banged her heels against the floor in the hope someone would hear. Something tickled her brain, almost a memory but not quite. An image of a soldier dressed in a Civil-War era uniform trying to speak to her, but she couldn't hear him over the rumble of an engine. She swung her feet harder, trying to make more noise so they'd shut off the machine. She wanted to hear what the apparition was saying.

The door opened and a light shined over her, stopping on her face. "Get me out of here," she screamed, afraid they'd leave her there to die. "Please don't leave me here with him." As the gloved hands of the fireman pulled the thin mattress put of the way, she heard another voice. One that immediately calmed her, as if she knew this person. The face looked vaguely familiar, but she didn't know him.

The snick of the door closing brought her back to the present to find her rescuer standing at the end of her bed, perusing her chart. Wishing it was her left arm in a cast, she awkwardly brushed the hair out of her eyes. "Hi. You're Mark, right?"

"Yes, Doctor Mark Fairfield. I treated you at the scene last night." He set the chart on the counter and turned to look at her. "How are you feeling this morning?"

"Not bad, other than the pain meds making me want to sleep.'

"Good. I wanted to check that you got some rest last night."

"Yeah, other than the nurse coming in every hour to check for a concussion." She frowned as she tried to adjust the pillows propping her up in the bed. "This bed isn't the most comfortable..."

"That's true. It looks like you're going to get released tomorrow afternoon. Do you have somewhere to go?"

"No, I'm not even sure where here is. I know I'm in Fairfield Corners, Indiana, but I have no clue where that is." She fiddled with the television remote as she replied, "I'm from Denver, so I could use a recommendation for a hotel until I get used to this thing." She knocked on the cast on her arm. "I don't know how I'm going to do this. I'm right-handed."

He turned and walked over to the window to look out over the parking lot. Something about this woman called out to his soul, he couldn't just send her to an anonymous hotel to fend for herself. "What if you stayed with me for a while? I have a big house on the other side of town. You'd have your own room, and I could help you until you feel confident enough to go home and care for yourself."

"Why would you do that for some woman you don't even know? I'm not sure if I would feel comfortable with that."

"Well, there is a bed and breakfast out near my house. The owner, Mrs. Dehaven, will take excellent care of you. It would be better than some chain hotel. If money is an issue, I can cover the cost of the room."

"Why are you being so nice when we've only just met?" She looked at him, as if trying to discover his secrets.

He sat in the chair next to the bed. "The moment I saw you tied up and bleeding in that truck camper, I knew you were important."

"Important how?"

"I have no idea, but I want to find out."

"Thank you for the offer but... I don't know, I'm not sure I can trust you."

Mark chuckled. "I'm the most boring, dependable guy you'll find. Just ask around."

Picking up the bag he'd set at the end of the bed, he handed it to her. "I took the liberty of having a friend pick up some clothes and stuff for you."

A surge of jealousy raced through her as she wondered if the friend was female and how close they were. *Where did that come from?* She didn't know this guy, so why should she care if he had a girlfriend? Shoving the almost overwhelming feeling down to a manageable level, she looked down at the cast on her arm. "Thank you, I appreciate it." She yawned. The pain meds had reduced the pain in her arm to a dull throb.

"You need to rest. I'll check back tomorrow and see if you've decided about the room."

"Okay," she murmured as her eyes drifted shut.

Chapter Four

As THE DOOR closed behind him, Mark wondered about Bette Watson. He'd offered to call her family but she'd said there was no one to worry about her.

Deputy Logan Miller walked up. "Hey, Mark. How's she doing?"

"She's doing well. The arm was a clean break and there's no sign of concussion. She'll probably be released tomorrow."

"That's good. I have some questions for her when she's up to it."

"She was drifting off to sleep a few minutes ago. Maybe in an hour or so?"

"I'll stop back later. Do you know if she has somewhere to stay?"

"I offered her my guest room until she feels ready to head back to Denver, but I don't think she's going to take me up on it."

"Are you sure about that? You know nothing about this woman."

"There's just something about her. I want to keep her close until I figure out what it is. Somehow, she's important."

"Fairfield Corners strikes again," Logan commented with a chuckle, referring to his almost life-long connection to his wife Cassie through his dreams. Fate was strong in the small Indiana town, bringing people together in unusual ways.

"Well, something drew me back here after six months in Indianapolis. Maybe I needed to be here for Bette Watson. We shall see."

Mark placed the chart into the rack at the nurse's station. "How's the boy doing?"

"Actually, Dane is why I stopped to talk to you. Cassie and I have applied to be the boy's foster parents and have him temporarily until Monday. We've been going through training and now here's this boy that needs a home. Is fate playing with us again? Anyway, I'm sure he's going to need someone to talk to about this whole thing, and I figured you might know of someone. You can see the pain in his eyes, though he's doing a pretty good job of hiding it."

"Sure, I know a couple of psychologists who might be a good fit. I'll text you their numbers." He tapped at his phone. "I bet Cassie is over the moon. I know how much she wanted more kids."

"She is, I just hope DCS approves the placement. She's already making plans and Vivi is following him around. I don't want either of my girls to be disappointed."

"I'm sure it will go through. You two will be terrific foster parents."

Logan's radio squawked, the dispatcher's voice calling for him.

"Duty calls. I'll talk to you later." Logan walked away as he replied to the dispatcher.

Mark returned to his empty house after his shift, figuring he'd better get the guest room ready in case Bette took him up on his offer. Luckily, the guest room was one of the first rooms he'd renovated so it was freshly painted, if a bit stark. There was a bed and a dresser, but nothing else. He remembered a set of night tables in the attic that would look good in the room.

After dumping the new sheets he'd purchased on his way home in the washer, he headed for the attic, the place of forgotten Fairfield treasures. Uncovering the night tables, he was glad to see they were in good condition and just needed a good cleaning. They were small enough he could maneuver them down the stairs without help.

When he picked up the first night table, he heard something sliding around in the drawer. Curious, he set it down and pulled the top drawer open, finding an ornately carved wooden box. Dusting it off, he was pleased to find an antique brush and comb set, engraved with a W. They must have belonged to his great grandmother Mary; her maiden name was Wilding. The set would look nice on the dresser. A small thing, but it would help the room feel more inviting.

Cleaned and polished, the night tables looked like they belonged in the room. He'd also found a portrait of his great grandmother, so he hung it above the bed. It didn't look quite right there but he was too tired to worry about it. The room was as ready as it was going to get, and he was tired and needed a nap.

The dream started out the same as before: *The house, the creek, their tree. Leaves rustled in the breeze, rattling like whispers. He waited anxiously as nine o'clock came and went with no sign of his love.*

Jeremiah Winston stepped out from behind a tree. "I should have known it was you. You think I didn't notice my daughter sneaking around?" He paced in front of Marcus, a pistol in his hand. "I told her, and now I'm telling you—my daughter will marry someone of my choosing, not some upstart Yankee. We are a proud Southern family, there is no way in hell I'm letting her run off with you."

Surprised to see her father as he was supposed to be on his way to Mobile, he stuttered, "Sir, I..."

"Leave. NOW. There is nothing for you here. Elizabeth is already married to someone suitable."

No, this could not be happening. His Lizzie married to someone else?

Mark's alarm rang, jolting him out of the dream. Overwhelming sadness filled his heart as he sat up and rubbed his hands down his face. The smell of the creek wafted through the air, as if his dream had become real. Maybe a hot shower would return his world to normal.

Toweling off, he glanced up at the mirror, surprised to discover a message on the foggy surface. "Find her."

The words faded, morphing into the face of his great grandfather as he'd looked in his dream: young and handsome.

Chapter Five

ELIZABETH HUMMED *as she brushed her hair. The brush in her hand part of the set her father had given her for her sixteenth birthday. She normally used the set that had been her mother's, but she'd given that to her soldier along with a spare dress and underthings. Today, all she had to take with her was her reticule. Soon she would be off on her new life with her love. He looked so dashing in his uniform, and she wished her father would see beyond the uniform and get to know the man who wore it. She was so tired of her father limiting her contact with anyone who didn't believe as rabidly in the Confederacy as he did. Sneaking around went against everything her mother had taught her about being a lady, but she would do whatever it took to be with her love.*

The day had dawned bright and sunny, matching her mood, but it had all gone quickly downhill. First, her father introduced her to some pompous plantation owner, stating that this is who she was to marry.

Now she was locked in her room, awaiting the summons for her unwanted wedding to this stranger.

The locked clicked before the door swung open.

"Elizabeth, it is time."

"No, Papa, I refuse to marry someone I don't know."

"Yes, you will. Your precious Yankee is gone. His Union army was more important to him than you are."

"No! You're lying." Thunder cracked and lightening flashed, as if mirroring her fury.

"I met him at your rendezvous spot down by the creek. He left without a fight when I told him you weren't coming."

"You told him I wasn't meeting him? How could you?"

"You will do as I say and marry Abraham Lewis. I made the mistake of marrying for love instead of following my family's wishes and look where it got me." He paced the length of the room and back, turning to look at his wayward daughter. "Everyone warned me that your mother was a witch, but I had to go my own way."

She couldn't get past the fact that Marcus had left her without even a goodbye. Her voice rising to rival the symphony of sound from the storm outside she cast the incantation she'd found in her mother's spell book, shouting, "I curse his name and all his descendants. They will never find lasting happiness."

Once she uttered those words, her mood improved and the storm subsided. Resigned to her fate, she bowed her head. "I'm ready, Papa. It's time to start my new life." Once they were away from her father, she would find a way to get to Marcus and find out why he'd betrayed her.

The dream lingered as she stretched, Elizabeth's anger a hard knot in her gut. As the feelings drifted away as if wisps of smoke, Bette thought maybe she needed to stay in Indiana for a while. She had nothing tying her to Denver other than her job and an apartment she hated. Maybe it was time for a fresh start. It was strange how the soldier in her dream resembled the handsome doctor.

Chapter Six

DISCHARGE PAPERWORK IN HAND, Mark wheeled Bette out the door of the hospital to his vehicle, a rust-covered 1972 Chevy pickup, its bed full of drywall.

"Sorry about the truck but I needed to pick up a load of supplies."

She slid into the seat, pleased to discover the interior was in much better shape than the outside. "No problem. It's not like I was expecting a limo or anything."

Bette stared out the window at the corn fields as they drove down the country road. "Wow, it's so flat."

"Welcome to Indiana. I'm sorry for how you ended up here, but I'm not sorry you are."

What, does he think I'm interested in him? She'd just met him two days ago when he discovered her in that truck's wreckage. She felt the anger rising again. *What is it about this guy?* For some reason she got angry every time he said something nice. He'd given her no reason to be mad, even going so far as to offer her a place to stay until she was ready to return home. Weird.

"So, what's all the drywall for?"

He smiled as he drove past a sign for the Fairfield Quarry and turned onto what looked like a private drive. "I'm restoring my great grandfather's home. I hope you don't mind; I need to stop and pick up a book I promised to loan Mrs. Dehaven."

Her eyes widened as he stopped in front of the house. "Wow, what a beautiful old home. I love old houses." She stared at the house for a moment. "Wait a minute, Fairfield. Didn't they say I was in Fairfield Corners? The town is named after your family?"

"Yes, the town grew here after my great-great grandfather started the quarry. He came here from Pennsylvania with his sons."

"Wow, I've never known anyone with their own town before."

"Well, it's not mine as in I don't own anything other than this house and the quarry. I do own a construction company in Fort Wayne."

"But still, to have a town named after your family. How do you have time to be a doctor?"

He reached over and opened his door. "It's no big deal. The quarry is just a hole in the ground full of water now and I have a manager that runs the construction company." He turned to get out of the truck. "Just give me a minute to go grab that book and I'll get you over to the bed and breakfast."

She put her hand on his arm. "Can I get a tour? It's so grand looking."

"Sure." Jumping out of the truck, he trotted over to the passenger side and opened the door. Holding out his hand, he helped her out of the truck and onto her feet. "Just take it slow, we're in no hurry."

"My legs are just fine, it's my arm that's broken," she replied as she slapped his hand away. Her face flushed red with embarrassment. "I'm so sorry, I don't know what got into me."

"It might be a reaction to the pain meds. They affect people differently." He led her up onto the porch.

She stood and stared out across the open expanse of the yard. "Wow, you've got a lot of space here. Don't you get lonely out here by yourself?"

"Not usually. I've been too busy renovating to be lonely. I like the quiet after a busy shift in the ER."

"Lead on. I can't wait to see the inside."

After they let their eyes adjust from the bright sunlight outside, Mark led her into the parlor.

"You did say you were in the process of restoring the house." She could see where the mudding and taping had been done in the hallway and parlor, the walls ready for some primer and then color. "Wow, looks like you've already gotten a lot accomplished."

"I have a crew that comes in on the weekends to do the major stuff." With his hand at her back, he steered her toward the kitchen. "I like to do the finish work myself."

She wandered from room to room. "Wow, that's a lot of drywall. Wasn't anything salvageable?"

"The house stood empty for over one hundred years, with only basic maintenance until I started renovations a couple of months ago. Just to warn you, people say it's haunted by the ghost of my great grandfather."

"Haunted? Oh, how exciting."

"I've seen a couple of things I can't explain but I'm not ready to say it's definitely haunted. Maybe he'll show himself to you."

"I'm fascinated by the idea of someone coming back to this world after they've died. What could be so important to them that they wouldn't leave this reality?"

"According to the stories handed down, he shut himself up in here after my great grandmother Mary died in childbirth. My grandfather was sent to live in town with the nanny." He took her hand and led her toward the staircase. "Ever since he died, no one has been able to live in this house for more than a couple of weeks until I moved in a month ago. For some reason, he hasn't bothered me."

"Sounds sad and romantic, shutting yourself away to grieve in private." She followed him up the stairs, wondering what the rooms looked like. Leading her down the hall, she watched as he avoided looking at the door to the left. Motioning to the room on the right, he urged her forward.

"This is the guest room. If the bed and breakfast doesn't work out, you are more than welcome to stay here." Opening the door, he let her enter first, walking around her to open the curtains. "I apologize, it's a bit stark."

Drawn to the dresser, Bette picked up the brush, comb, and hand mirror, looking at each and then carefully setting them back down. "This set looks antique."

"From the W engraved into the design, I believe it belonged to my great grandmother. I thought it might make the room feel a little lived in. Silly, huh?"

As soon as she'd touched the brush, she'd known he was wrong. The set hadn't belonged to this Mary, it had belonged to Elizabeth. Why couldn't he see that? "No, I like it. It's a nice touch. Who is Elizabeth?"

"Elizabeth? I don't know of anyone with that name."

"I just have a feeling the set was important to someone named Elizabeth. Maybe Mary had a sister?"

"Not that I know of, but we don't know much about her family. I know there's some old trunks up in the attic. Maybe I'll take a look this weekend when I have some free time."

"I'd like to help. I know I can't do any heavy lifting, but I can help you go through any papers you find." For some reason, she had to see what was up in the attic. She wanted to jump up and do it right that moment, but her arm was starting to ache.

He noticed the pain in her eyes, his doctor instincts on high alert. "Looks like you could use a pain pill and some rest. The trunks haven't moved in years and will be there waiting when you're up to it. I left your prescription in the truck. Let me go get it and then we can continue the tour if you feel up to it. Why don't you sit down, and I'll be right back."

When he left the room, she returned to the dresser and picked up the brush again. *How in the world do I know this didn't belong to Mary? And why is Elizabeth's brush set here in this house?*

Mark returned with a glass of water, handing it to her along with two white pills. "Here you go." He watched, mesmerized as she swallowed the pills, his attention focused on the curve of her cheek. It looked so familiar.

The tooting of a car horn took his attention away from her. "That must be Cassie. She's bringing over some things you can borrow."

"Oh, I couldn't accept anything else. I've got money, it's just in Denver."

"Don't worry about it. You can call your bank later today and arrange to get some money transferred here."

"Is there a Merit Bank here in town?"

"Not in Fairfield Corners, but I believe there is a branch about twenty-minutes from here in Fort Wayne, ."

"Oh, that's good. Can you take me there tomorrow?"

"Sure. Will they give you any problems since you don't have any ID?"

"Oh, I didn't think about that."

"We'll figure something out."

They heard the front door open. "Mark? Where are you?"

He stepped out into the hall and looked down the stairs. "We're up here."

After a few moments, Ragan appeared in the doorway "Hi, you must be Bette. I'm Ragan." She turned to Mark. "Cassie is on a call with DCS so I offered to bring this stuff out to you. She picked up some basics. When you're feeling better, we can all go on a proper shopping spree." She pulled clothes out of the shopping bags at her feet. "Just let me know if things don't fit. Now, let's get you into something comfortable, you look like you need to get some sleep. Mark, why don't you go unload the truck or something."

Bette noticed the way Mark looked at Ragan, his look of longing indicating he may feel something more than friendship for her.

"Fine, I know when I'm not wanted.," he said with a grin.

Once he'd walked out of the room, she couldn't hold back her curiosity. "So, I noticed the way Mark looks at you. What's the story there? Any chance for the two of you?" Even as she asked the question, she hoped the answer was no. She'd only met the doctor a couple of days before, but something about him called to her soul. Her attraction to him was so strong that sometimes she felt almost jealous of the people he knew. *How can I be jealous over someone I've just met?*

"Oh, no. We dated for a while, but it wasn't meant to be. That story requires wine and more time than we have today. Let's see if these clothes are the right size."

After helping Bette change into a clean pair of jeans and a soft T-shirt, Ragan carried the bags out of the room, her eyes avoiding the closed door across the hall. They trooped down the stairs and out onto the porch. "I'm glad everything fit. Cassie guessed at the sizes."

"Did something happen in that room across the hall from the bedroom we were in? I saw you averting your eyes as if you couldn't bear to even look at the door. Mark did the same thing when he took me upstairs to the guest room."

"Mark's brother died in that room. He's still coming to terms with that."

"Oh, wow. I'm glad I mentioned it to you instead of him. How awful."

"It's part of that story I told you required wine."

"I'm always up for a good bottle of wine. Not that I'm a drunk or anything..." Bette blushed. "Geez, I must be more tired than I thought." She shoved her dirty clothes into the empty bag and picked it up. "Thank you for bringing the clothes, and please, thank Cassie for me too." Her attention wandered to Mark, his sweat-soaked T-shirt stuck to him like a second skin as he lifted a sheet of drywall out of the truck. He was close enough she could see his muscles flex as he carried the heavy materials toward the porch steps. "Oh, my," she whispered.

They stepped back to give him room to maneuver the drywall into the house. He stepped back out onto the porch, wiping at his forehead with the bottom of his shirt.

Both of them stared at the glimpse of toned abs. "You know, a girl could do worse than a good-looking doctor," Ragan whispered.

Bette blushed. She hadn't meant for her interest in the handsome doctor to be quite so obvious. "I'm only here for a few days, then I'm going back home."

"That's too bad. You're the first woman he's shown an interest in since he came back from Indianapolis."

"Interested? In me? I don't think so. He just feels sorry for me being injured so far away from home. Besides, you didn't see how he looked at you."

"That's his 'what could have been' look. I think it's more habit for him than anything else at this point. He needs someone in his life. I worry about him all alone in this big old house."

Mark returned to the porch. "That was the last of the drywall. I've got a few more things to bring in, then I'll be ready to take you over to the bed and breakfast."

Ragan offered, "I can take her over and get her settled in."

"No, I'll do it. Just let me finish up and put on a clean shirt."

Once he stepped back toward the truck, Ragan leaned in closer to Bette and whispered, "See? Told you. He's interested."

"Maybe you're right. Thanks for the pep talk." She grabbed Ragan's hand, surprised at how close she felt to this relative stranger. "I hope I see you again before I leave."

"Have Mark bring you over to the pub for dinner, and you can meet my husband."

As much as she liked Ragan, she was still relieved to hear she was married. "I'll do that."

Ragan drove off as Mark returned to the porch wearing a clean shirt. "You look tired. I called yesterday and reserved your room. It should be ready for you when we get there."

She tried to hide her yawn behind her hand. "I could use a nap."

"Well then, let's go get you settled into your room." He put his hand against the small of her back and motioned her toward the vehicles parked to the side of the house. Walking over to a high-end, late-model sedan, he clicked the button on the fob to unlock the doors before he opened the passenger door and helped her sit.

She settled into the leather seat and sniffed, "Oooh, new car smell."

He laughed. "I just got it last week, so it hasn't worn off yet." He rubbed his hands over the steering wheel. "I still marvel at it. This is my first brand-new car, ever."

"What? I thought you came from money?" She looked at him with surprise.

"Yeah, but Dad wanted us to learn the value of a dollar, so we had to work for what we wanted." He smiled sadly. "He would have liked you."

She didn't know what to say to that, so she stared out the window as he drove down to the road.

A short time later, he pulled up in front of a large Victorian house, the sign in front declaring it the Fairfield Corners Bed & Breakfast. The rocking chairs on the wraparound porch looked like the perfect place to while away an afternoon with a glass of wine and a good book.

"Oh my," she breathed. "It's gorgeous."

"Mrs. DeHaven will take good care of you."

She looked at Mark as he helped her out of the car, his hand warm around hers. *Why do I feel this connection with a man I barely know?*

He led her up the porch steps to stand in front of an older lady.

"This must be the poor dear," Mrs. DeHaven said as she looked at Bette, frowning at the cast on her arm. "Don't you worry about a thing. I've got your room ready for you." She turned and walked toward the open door. "Mark, I put her in Room three at the top of the stairs. The door is open, and the key is on the dresser. Please show her up to her room and I'll get the tea ready."

Mark stared at her retreating back and chuckled. "See? She has everything under control. All her guests are family to her."

Bette yawned again. "Tea sounds lovely, but a nap sounds even better. Will she be offended if I head upstairs instead?"

"I'll explain it to her. Don't worry about it."

After climbing the stairs, she marveled at the room before her. A large four-poster bed draped in a beautiful handmade quilt dominated the room. To the right of the bed was a fireplace with a couple of chairs in front of it, and there was a small closet to the right of the bed. Another door led to an en suite bath. Atop the dresser was the television, the remote, and a room key. "This is perfect," she said as she tested the firmness of the mattress. "Thank you so much for arranging this. I'll pay you back as soon as I get some money transferred."

"It was my pleasure." He set the bag holding the few things Ragan had brought over on the bench at the foot of the bed. "We'll go into Fort Wayne tomorrow and get your banking figured out. I'll call you later this evening to set up a time."

She watched him walk out of the room and close the door softly behind him. Once he was gone, she kicked off her shoes and crawled onto the bed, sighing at the softness of the pillows. Within a few moments, she was asleep.

Mark walked into the parlor and found Mrs. DeHaven fussing over a tray with a teapot and three cups along with a plate of her homemade cookies.

"Your young lady isn't joining us?" she asked when she noticed Mark walk into the room alone.

"No, she's exhausted and needed to sleep." He sat across from her and motioned to the teapot. "Is the tea ready?"

With a glance at her watch, she nodded. "Yes. I'm sorry she won't be joining us. I heard about the accident. It's hard to believe something like that happened in our sleepy little town."

She looked up when the front door opened, smiling when she saw it was Cassie.

"Come, sit and have tea with us," she said as she motioned to the seat next to Mark.

"Tea sounds wonderful, Mrs. DeHaven," Cassie replied as she sat. "I just wanted to check on Bette. Ragan said she was fine, but I wanted to see for myself."

Mark sighed, "She's fine. She's in her room taking a nap."

Mrs. DeHaven poured tea and passed around the sugar bowl. "Now, Mark, I hear you were there at the accident scene. That must have been exciting."

Chapter Seven

Dust motes floated in the air as Mark pulled the box closer to Bette, making sure she could reach the papers inside before he turned back to the jumble of trunks in the far corner of the attic. He'd planned on taking her into Fort Wayne to see the zoo, but the stormy weather changed his plans. She'd been excited when he mentioned going through some of the things up in the attic, but he hadn't said anything about wanting to search for any mention of the mysterious Lizzie from his dream. Through Mark's dreams—and a few scary encounters—Great Grandfather Marcus Fairfield had made known his wish for Mark to find her, going so far as to write "Lizzie" on the steam-covered bathroom mirror.

"I wanted to take you somewhere fun for your last day here. It's too bad the weather didn't cooperate."

"To me, this is just as much fun as going to a zoo. I love going through old stuff 'cause you never know what you'll find."

After going through three of the four trunks and finding nothing more than some old dresses, he was resigned to the day being a bust. Huffing out a sigh, he was surprised to find the last trunk was locked. Smaller than the others, he wondered why it was the only one locked. Running his hands through his hair, he remembered finding a ring of old skeleton keys the day before. He been surprised to find them as he'd emptied the desk a couple of weeks back, and they weren't in there then.

The rain outside raised the humidity in the house, making the attic a sauna. He'd tried using a fan but that had stirred up so much dust it became impossible to see across the room. Man, he really needed to bring the vacuum and cleaning supplies up here and get rid of some of the grime. He gulped down the last of the water in his bottle. "You need some more water? I can't believe how hot it is up here today."

Bette looked up at him, shaking her bottle. "Yeah, I'm almost out." She handed the bottle to him. "Did you know your grandfather never lived in this house after he was sent away as a baby? By the time he graduated from college, he'd already married your grandmother and she wanted nothing to do with this house." She picked up the journal she'd been reading from. "According to your grandmother's journal, she hated this house the first time she saw it and refused to set foot inside when they arrived here. She forced your grandfather to rent a motel room in town until they could have another house built."

"I remember her telling me about that day, but I never knew if it was true. She was already in the early stages of Alzheimer's by then. The other house burned down when I was a boy." He wiped at the sweat on his forehead. "Why don't we go downstairs and cool off? This stuff isn't going anywhere and its lunch time. You hungry?"

"That sounds good." She stood and brushed at the dust on her shorts.

Grasping her hand, he helped her step around the mess they'd made, the clothes and books from the trunks spread out across the floor. As always, he was surprised by the zing of electricity he felt when he first touched her hand, zapping through his system like a firefly flitting through the dark. "Lunch is just sandwiches, so I hope that's okay. I had planned to have lunch somewhere in Fort Wayne today, but our choices are limited since we stayed in. It's either sandwiches or we wait while I go pick up something at a drive-through."

"Sandwiches are fine. You know, you don't need to keep taking me out to eat. Meals are included with my room at the bed and breakfast. And Mrs. DeHaven is a wonderful cook."

He carefully led her down the stairs, making sure she felt secure. He remembered what it felt like to have his arm in a cast, the weight of the plaster making him feel off kilter. "Go ahead and sit down, and I'll make the sandwiches. I've got ham or turkey, I think."

"Turkey, if you have it, with mayo please."

"Got it. Cheese?"

"Of course."

He piled the sandwich fixings on the counter and returned to the fridge. I've only got white bread. I hope that's okay. I know it's bad, but I just love white, squishy bread."

She smiled. "My thoughts exactly. It's my guilty pleasure, along with diet soda."

"Diet soda? You know how bad that is for you, don't you?"

"I know it's full of chemicals, but I love it. That's me, living on the edge."

He set a plate in front of her, a sandwich and potato salad taking up most of it. "If you don't like anything, let me know."

"It looks yummy." As she ate, she wondered about his life. Why was he single? He was a good-looking guy with a great job.

"What? Do I have something on my face?" he asked as she stared at him.

"No. Just wondering why you're still single." She frowned as she contemplated possible reasons.

"I've been in love, but it didn't work out." He stood and picked up their empty plates. "The Fairfield family isn't very lucky in love. If we find it, it's either fleeting or someone dies."

"I get it if you don't want me to know you're involved. It's really none of my business," she snapped as she pushed herself away from the table. The thought of him having a girlfriend pissed her off.

He stared after her, his expression showing his confusion.

She strode out of the house and onto the porch, her anger swelling. Thunder cracked as the rain poured down. Fat drops beat against the porch roof, drowning out all other sounds. She let the noise sooth her as she stared out into the trees across the open expanse of the yard.

As the rain lessened, she heard the notes of a familiar song, one that she'd heard recently on the radio. The song reached into her soul and lightened her mood, her thoughts turning to the reason for her anger. Where did it come from? *Why does the thought of this handsome doctor being involved with someone make me want to murder someone?*

"You okay out there?"

"Yeah. I'm sorry for flying off the handle like that. I don't know what's wrong with me lately."

"You look tired. Maybe we should stop for the day." He leaned against the doorjamb.

"No, I'm fine. Must be the weather."

He held his hand out to her. "You ready to go back up to the attic? I bet the key for that trunk is on the ring I found a couple of days ago. I'll grab it and we can head back upstairs."

He followed her up the staircase, his mind racing with thoughts of lost treasures found.

Pulling the ring of keys he'd found in the desk near the stairs leading to the attic from his pocket, he tried the most likely-looking one in the lock. It was odd it was the only trunk that was locked. With a twist of his wrist, the lock clicked.

Pushing the lid of the trunk up, he held his breath. Would the contents lead them to the mysterious Lizzie? He stared down at a small bag and leather-bound journal. "I wonder what's so special about this that it needed to be locked up?"

"What did you find?" She peered into the trunk and poked at the bag. Something in the bag called to her. "Can I see what's in there?"

"Sure." He handed the bag to her, returning to the trunk to pick up the journal. Thunder boomed as his fingertips touched the book, rattling the windows. With a pop, the light bulbs went dark. "Well, crap. There goes the power. Let's take this stuff downstairs where it's brighter."

"Sounds like a plan."

He stumbled over toward the door. "Let me go get a flashlight so you don't trip over anything. Will you be okay up here by yourself for a couple of minutes?"

Without the light, the atmosphere of the attic had changed. "Sure," she replied.

Thunder continued to rumble as she waited for Mark to return. Her eyelids drooped. Maybe she should have agreed to a nap before they returned to the attic.

The rain lashed at the windows as she listened for footsteps. Elizabeth folded the dress and placed it in her valise. Returning to her dressing table, she stroked the silver hairbrush. "Oh Mama, am I doing the right thing? I don't want to go against Papa's wishes, but I love him." Picking up the brush and the matching mirror, she placed them carefully in the bag. Replacing the set with another out of a drawer, she heard the distinctive sound of her father's footsteps. She shoved the bag under the bed and sat at the dressing table. As her door opened, she picked up the brush as if she'd been using it to smooth her hair.

"Elizabeth, I would like to speak to you in the parlor."

"Yes, Papa." Setting the brush down, she stood and followed her father down the stairs.

"Tomorrow, Mr. Lewis will be dining with us for supper. Please inform the cook and make sure everything will be in order." He paced the length of the room and turned back to face her. "I will be leaving on my trip to Alabama directly after dinner."

"Is there going to be a war, Papa?"

"Who put such an idea in your head? It's nothing for you to worry about." He resumed his pacing. "It's high time you were married and in a home of your own. Therefore, you will marry Mr. Lewis directly before I leave on my trip."

"But, Papa, I..."

"But nothing. As your father, it is my job to find you a suitable husband."

Elizabeth fought to maintain her cool façade. "Yes, Papa."

"You may return to your room."

As she trudged up the stairs, she wondered how her soldier would feel about waiting another day before they left for Indiana. With her father leaving, it would be the perfect time for her to slip away, giving them enough time to get out of Georgia before anyone would be looking for her.

A clap of thunder woke Bette from her dream. Wow, the dreams were getting more vivid.

The creak of a step heralded Mark's return to the attic, the beam of a flashlight lighting his way. "Sorry it took so long, I had to find fresh batteries."

"That's okay, I was just sitting up here listening to the storm. I love hearing the rain hitting the roof, it's actually quite soothing."

He handed her the light, "Here, you light the way and I'll carry this stuff downstairs."

As she followed Mark down the stairs her fingers itched to dig through the contents of the bag. Something in there was important, she could feel it.

The living room was bright, the sun shining down on the earth through a break in the clouds made the water droplets sparkle. The world outside looked fresh and clean.

Placing the items on the coffee table, Mark turned to help Bette get settled on the couch. She reached for the bag when Mark's phone rang.

He pulled his cell out of his pocket. "It's the hospital, I've got to take this. "Don't open the bag without me," he said with a grin as he walked out of the room.

"Argh, okay. I'll wait." She poked at the bag, wondering what was inside.

She ran her hands over the journal, surprised at the waves of longing that rolled through her. Picking up the book, she let her mind wander. "So much unrequited love and sadness, so alone," she whispered.

Mark returned to the room as she wiped at a tear. "Hey, what's wrong?"

She held up the journal. "Whoever wrote this was so sad. Can't you feel it?"

"You started reading it without me?"

"Oh, no. I haven't even opened it. I can feel the sadness rolling off it in waves. I've never experienced anything like it."

He looked from her back to the journal. "You didn't tell me you could 'feel' things."

"I can't. At least, I never have before I came here."

Picking up the book, his hands brushed hers and the zing of electricity was stronger this time. "Well, let's see who this journal belonged to…" Opening the front cover, he was pleased to see his grandfather's name inscribed inside. "Oh wow, it's my great grandfather's. Maybe now I can discover why he's haunting this house."

"So, you've seen him?"

"Yeah. He's been telling me to find his Lizzie. No one in the family knows who she was, my great grandmother's name was Mary."

"Oooh, a mystery. How exciting." She wondered if this Lizzie had anything to do with her dreams. Lizzie was a nickname for Elizabeth…

"Can we open the bag now? I'm curious to see what's inside."

"Go ahead." He smiled at her excitement.

She unhooked the clasp and pulled it open. On top was a dress, and she was shocked to discover it was the one from her dream. *What is Elizabeth's bag doing in Mark's great grandfather's attic?* Should she mention her dreams to him?

"Just a dress. Is there anything else in the bag?"

Reaching in the bag, she pulled out some papers. She carefully unfolded one, the paper yellowed and brittle with age.

"What does it say?"

She cleared her throat. "My Dearest Lizzie."

"Lizzie? Marcus's Lizzie? We found her."

"What do you mean Marcus's Lizzie? How is she connected?"

"I think he was in love with her before he met my great grandmother Mary. He's been appearing to me insisting that I find his Lizzie. Maybe now he'll let me sleep in peace."

She had to tell him about her daydreams. "This is going to sound weird, but I've been having dreams about the woman who owns this dress. I recognized it from my dream as soon as I pulled it out of the bag."

"You've been dreaming about Lizzie?"

"Her name is Elizabeth Hamilton. I didn't connect her to your great grandfather. She usually thinks of him as her soldier."

"We have a name, so we can do a search for her. I wonder why it's so important that I find her now?"

"As much as I want to stay and help, I need to go home and get back to my real life." She stood and picked up her empty water bottle. "I need some more water. All that dust upstairs dried out my throat." She took a step toward the kitchen and then turned to look at him. "Do you need another?" she asked as she waggled the bottle in her hand.

"Sure," he replied absently as he examined the dress, his mind on the mysterious Lizzie.

Bette reached into the fridge for a couple of bottles of water, her mind whirling with anger as Lizzie's voice taunted her, *"See? He doesn't care that you're leaving. He doesn't deserve your interest."*

"He didn't say that," she muttered to herself. "Get out of my head!"

"Who are you talking to?" Mark asked from the doorway.

"Just myself," she answered and handed him one of the bottles. "I do that sometimes," she muttered as disappointment rushed through her. Maybe she'd been mistaken about him.

Bette stood on the porch with her coffee, staring out across the road in front of the bed and breakfast. Her bag was packed with the few things she'd purchased on her shopping trip with Cassie and Ragan. Sad to be leaving, she was still excited to be headed home. But what should she do about Mark? She was definitely attracted to the handsome doctor, but the day before he'd seemed indifferent to her.

Forget him, he's not worth your time.

She hated the voice in her head that contradicted everything she felt. A voice that had first popped up after she'd arrived in Fairfield Corners. Lost in thought, she didn't notice Mark's car pulling up in front of the porch.

"Hey," she heard as someone touched her arm.

"What?" She was surprised to see Mark standing next to her.

"Must have been some heavy thinking going on," he said with a smile.

"Oh, yeah." She dumped the dregs of her coffee into the flowerbed. "Is it nine thirty already?"

"Not quite."

"I'll just go up and get my bag." Mark's hand on her arm stopped her mid-step. "What?"

"Did I say something to upset you?" He asked, his eyes searching her face. "If I did, I'm sorry."

"No, it's nothing. Just sad I'm leaving, I guess." Her hand on the door, she turned back to him. "Want some coffee? Mrs. DeHaven made muffins this morning." She laughed at his groan. "I know! Don't tell anyone, but I ate three of them yesterday morning."

"Mum's the word." He started up the steps. "Let's get your bag and then we can gorge ourselves on baked goods before we leave. Her muffins are way better than anything you can get at the airport."

"Go get a muffin. All I've got is the one bag." She left him standing at the base of the stairs, staring after her.

Setting her bag on the floor near the door, she peeked in the dining room. Empty. Following the sound of voices, she walked into the kitchen and smiled when she caught Mark with his mouth full of muffin, looking guilty.

Grinning, she reached for a muffin. "How many is that? Two? Three?"

Sipping his coffee he swallowed and replied, "Two, but I definitely have room for a third."

Mrs. DeHaven picked up the empty platter and replaced it with one piled with muffins. "Now, eat up."

After hugs with Mrs. DeHaven and a few tears, Bette followed Mark out to his car. She couldn't believe her time in Indiana was already at an end. It had only been a few days, but the small town had begun to feel more like home than Denver ever had.

She watched the green of the corn slip past the windows as Mark sped along the highway. The miles rushed past, taking her time in Indiana with them. The week she'd spent in Fairfield Corners felt like so much more than just an interlude in her normal life. Spending time with Mark and meeting his friends made her realize how empty her life was in Denver. She already missed the feeling of belonging, and she hadn't even left the state.

Bette looked at Mark when she felt the car stop. "What? Are we there already?" she asked as she looked around her, dismayed to discover she'd spent the entire twenty-minute drive lost in her own thoughts.

"Yeah." Mark smiled at her and pulled her bag from the back seat.

Well, it was time, and she didn't know what to say. She hurried around the car and stood facing Mark.

"Now, you've got everything? Your ticket? A book? Money for snacks?" He held her bag out to her.

"Yes, dear," she replied sarcastically as she took the bag. It hit her that she was going to have to say goodbye. How was she supposed to do that without sobbing? Averting her eyes, she unzipped her bag and checked that she had her ticket. "Well, I guess this is it."

"You could stay a few more days. I've got that room if you don't want to spend the money for the B & B."

She reached over and cupped his jaw. "I wish I could, but I've got to get back to my life." Pulling the strap of her bag further up her shoulder, she stepped back. "Thanks for…everything." She turned and hurried into the terminal, not wanting Mark to see her tears.

Mark stared after her, only getting back in the car when someone honked their horn.

Chapter Eight

BETTE WATCHED out the window as the ground rushed up at the underbelly of the plane, the tires making contact with the earth. She was finally home.

The mountains called to her, reminding her why she loved living in Denver. But now it felt different, as if she was visiting instead of coming home. Weird. She'd only been in Indiana for a week, so why did Denver suddenly not feel like home?

As she waited to exit the aircraft, she wondered what Mark was doing. Knowing he was scheduled to be on shift at the hospital, she sent him a text letting him know she'd arrived safely instead of calling. It hadn't even been a full day and she already missed him.

The stewardess helped her get her carryon out of the overhead bin. "If you need any more help, please let one of us know."

"Thank you. I've got it from here."

Settling the strap of her bag on her shoulder, she strode toward the exit. She was surprised to see a uniformed driver holding a sign with her name on it. "I'm Bette Watson, but I think there's been a mistake. I didn't order a car."

"No mistake, ma'am. Mr. Bricklin sends his regards."

Mark had taken her to The Corner Pub for dinner after they'd spent the day digging through the trunks in his attic. Finding his great grandfather's journal had been cause for a small celebration. She'd been surprised to find out Ragan was married to Adam Bricklin. Slightly starstruck, it hadn't taken Adam long to put her at ease. And the kids, especially Skylar, running up to them yelling "Uncle Mark!" had melted her heart. She watched as Mark talked with the boy and knew he needed to have kids of his own.

Riding through downtown Denver in a limo felt like a dream. All too quickly, she was standing in front of her apartment building with her car in its assigned parking spot. She turned to find the limo driver standing next to her, her purse and a manila envelope in his hand.

"Mr. Bricklin took the liberty of arranging for your car to be delivered and for your locks to be changed. The police recovered your purse, and everything seemed to be intact, but Mr. Bricklin thought it would be prudent to change the locks."

She opened the envelope to find a keyring with her car keys and two shiny new house keys.

"This is too much." With tears in her eyes, she punched in Ragan's cell number, waiting patiently while it rang. "Ragan, do you know what your husband did?" As she listened to Ragan laugh, she decided she needed to consider returning to Indiana. As much as she loved Denver, she'd found something *more* in the small Indiana town—family.

"He told me this morning. That's just the type of guy he is."

"You hang onto him, he's a keeper. When I come back, I'm going to make him my famous devil's food cake."

"So, you're coming back? Permanently? I hope it's soon."

"At least for a visit. When I get my life back to normal, I'll see about taking some time off. Don't tell Mark, I want to surprise him." As much as she looked forward to spending more time with her new friend, she ached to be near Mark again. Weird, as they hadn't even kissed. As much as she missed the small Indiana town, she wasn't ready to commit to a permanent move—not yet anyway.

Mark was confused by Bette. One day she was sweet and happy to spend time with him. Others, it was as if she was another person who was angry at him. Oh well, it didn't make a difference since she'd gone back to her home and job in Denver. Even with the uncertainty of her moods, he missed her. They'd connected in a way that had him wondering about hospitals in Denver. It was hard to believe she'd only left that morning.

Marcus had popped in the previous night, seeming to watch Mark as he sanded drywall. The dust swirled, moving through the apparition. After he faded away, Mark had found the word Lizzie written in the drywall dust coating the floor.

"Oh, so just finding out who she was isn't enough?" He felt silly talking to an empty room, but the flickering lights indicated his ancestor was listening. "Okay, I'll see if Anna can find out what happened to her. Happy?"

The lights burned brighter for a moment before returning to their normal brightness. Currently in the middle of a shift, he was going through the motions and missing Bette. The urge to take her in his arms and kiss her had been strong as they sat in the drop-off lane at the Fort Wayne airport. Getting out of the car, he'd stood waiting as she walked around the front of the vehicle.

"I'll call you when I land. Thanks for everything." After a brief hug, she turned and made her way into the terminal.

Mark had stared after her, turning back to his car feeling as if he'd just said goodbye to her forever. He toyed with the idea of running into the airport after her, but a car honking behind his had squashed that idea.

Grumbly and moody, he plodded through his day until he received her text that she'd landed in Denver. Starting and stopping a reply, he grimaced at himself. No matter what he typed, it sounded corny. He was surprised to get a second text about ten minutes after the first.

I'm riding home in a limo thanks to Adam. I feel like royalty!

Slightly jealous he hadn't thought of that himself, he texted back.

Glad you made it home safely. Hope to see you soon.

He finished his shift in a much better mood.

The next evening, Mark stifled a yawn as he finished his notes on a chart, thankful he was back to working at the Fairfield County hospital.

The five minute drive home was much better than the twenty-minute drive from the Fort Wayne location. As soon as he notified the charge nurse he was off shift, he headed toward his car. Checking his phone, he was pleased to discover a text from Anna.

Found Elizabeth. Tracking descendants. Emailing info. More later.

He was going to owe his friend a huge favor. She'd only been searching for a couple of days, and had already found her.

He pulled up his email and opened the attachment.

The image was a copy of a marriage certificate. Elizabeth Hamilton married Abraham Lewis in 1861, around the start of the Civil War. It was surreal seeing her name written on the page. Lizzie was a real person, not just a figment of his imagination. As he drove home, he wondered how Marcus would react. Would it be enough to let the ghost of his ancestor finally rest easily?

It looked like every single light in the house was on as he pulled up and parked near the porch steps. Did Marcus already know that Anna had found his long-lost love?

The front door flew open before he could grab the doorknob. Stepping into the house, he watched the ghost of his great grandfather fade away before reappearing in a different spot in the room. "I take it you know my friend discovered Lizzie married and moved to Virginia?"

Mark puttered around the kitchen, putting together a dinner of leftovers. As he ate, the lights continued to flicker. "Okay, I get it. You're excited. Now please, stop with the lights. It's giving me a headache."

The lights dimmed to their normal brightness. "Thank you." He was glad no one was around to hear him talking to a ghost. Thoughts of Bette weighed heavily on his mind. Was she happy in Denver? What would she do if he showed up on her doorstep?

His phone buzzed, bringing him out of his musings and back to the present. Smiling at the text notification, he unlocked his phone and opened the texting app.

Bette: Missing you and your little town. How is everyone?

Mark: We're all fine—missing you, as well. Sky was asking where you were. You made quite an impression on him.

Bette: Give him a hug for me.

Mark: Will do. How's the arm?
Bette: Aches a little but it's fine.
Mark: You know I'm only a phone call away.

He waited for a reply and was disappointed when his phone remained silent.

Bette stared at her phone, conflicted. It had only been a couple of days and she was trying to resume her old life. Resisting the urge to call him, she made a deal with herself: if she still wanted—no needed—to talk to him after a week, then she'd call. It was time to get back to real life. Tomorrow was her first day back to work, and she hoped her boss didn't make a big deal about it. The time she'd spent in Indiana had been wonderful, but she had a plan that didn't include a handsome doctor or a quirky, small, Indiana town. Her dream was to buy out her boss and expand the business on the internet. Bette's Beautiful Things would specialize in antiques and one-of-a-kind gifts.

Digging through the trunks in Mark's home had been so much fun as they searched for information on the mysterious Lizzie. Even though they hadn't lived in the house, it had become the repository of all the Fairfield family's forgotten treasures. They'd only gone through the trunks at one end of the attic, and there were a multitude of boxes they hadn't yet touched. Her heart raced at the thought of seeing the handsome doctor again. Maybe it would take some time to convince him to let her inventory what he had and buy some of the items. She liked the idea, it gave her an excuse to go back to Fairfield Corners, and back to Mark.

Chapter Nine

TWO MONTHS LATER…

Bette disconnected the call and dropped her phone on the bed next to her. She yawned and stretched, wincing when she checked the time. Three in the morning! They'd been talking for over three hours. Talking to Mark about her day made her wish he was there with her, which was silly. She'd only been in Indiana for a week, certainly not long enough to have such intense feelings for the handsome doctor.

With a sigh, she picked up her phone and plugged it into the charger. She'd have to get through her day on four hours of sleep again. They drifted closer with each phone call. The calls ended up lasting hours, as neither of them wanted to be the first to say goodbye. At least she'd been able to sleep since the strange dreams had disappeared as soon as she'd returned to Denver.

She unlocked the door and punched in the alarm code on the pad by the door. Flipping switches, the lights came on, bringing the shelves of gifts into the day. She loved mornings in the store when she would rearrange stock and create pleasing displays. Hanging her purse on its hook in the storeroom, she turned to boxes that had arrived the previous day. She loved unpacking the boxes and discovering the treasures her boss had unearthed. It was almost as satisfying as her own trips to buy items for the store.

She poked her head out of the storeroom when she heard the tinkle of the bell over the door.

"Bette, I'm here. Sorry I'm late." her boss Donna Blye called out.

"No problem."

"Before we get going for the day, I need to talk to you." She walked past Bette to the small office next to the storeroom. "Come on in and sit down."

Bette returned the figurine in her hand to the open box and followed her into the tiny office, taking a seat in the chair in front of the desk.

"I wanted you to be the first to know I've decided to close the store."

"Close the store? I thought sales were good…"

Donna opened a file folder and shuffled through the papers. She pulled one out of the stack and handed it to Bette. "This is my asking price for you to buy me out." She waited a beat and continued. "We've talked before about you eventually buying my stock. Well, I've decided it's time for me to retire and move closer to my grandbabies."

Bette stared at the paper in her hand. "Wow, I wasn't expecting this." Her mind whirled with the possibilities. "Would I also be able to take over the lease?" As she said it an idea popped into her head. Was it doable, she wondered? Nothing was holding her here in Denver…

"Unfortunately, no. The mall has a waiting list for this space."

"Actually, that's perfect. I want to relocate out of state and run things online, then set up a physical store later." She stared at the amount again, it was higher than she'd expected. "Are you sure the buyout will be this much?" she asked, wondering if there was any wiggle room in that figure.

"I discussed this with my accountant, and this is a fair offer for the inventory. I hope we can come to an agreement. I know you love the business as much as I do. You've been with me since I opened the store, and you're more than just an employee to me."

Bette looked down at her hand, not wanting Donna to see her eyes filling with tears. Blinking rapidly, she looked back up.

"Take some time to think about it. There's still two months on my lease, so you have some time."

Bette stood as Donna walked around the desk. She gasped when her boss's arms went around her and pulled her into a hug. "I'm going to miss you, Bette."

"I'll miss you, too." She stepped back toward the door. "I better get that stock out on the shelves." She turned back and continued, "I'll let you know my decision by the end of the week." Her thoughts on the possibilities, she returned to the box and picked up the figurine to place it on the shelf.

Chapter Ten

ONE MONTH LATER...

Bette perused the online rental listings for Fort Wayne. Purchasing a property just wasn't in her budget. She'd looked in Fairfield Corners and had even called a real-estate agent, but there was nothing available. She'd been hoping to find something in the small town, but it looked like she would have to settle for the bigger city nearby. Clicking on a listing, she was pleased to discover it was a single-family dwelling on the west side of Fort Wayne. An older, three-bedroom home, it was the perfect size for her. She put down a deposit to hold the rental until she arrived in Indiana. She'd make a final decision when she toured the property.

Later that afternoon, she made a reservation at a Fort Wayne hotel and packed up her laptop. It was time for her to get on the road. Everything she owned was packed into a U-Haul with a tow-dolly attached to the back for her car.

Three days of driving had taken its toll. She was tired and it was time for dinner. Pulling into Fort Wayne, she followed her GPS to the hotel. Once she was in her room, she looked up the number for the closest pizza delivery and ordered dinner. She wanted nothing more than to unhook her car and head to Fairfield Corners, but she was tired and had a phone date with Mark. She'd have to be careful not to let on that she was in Fort Wayne. She wanted the move to Indiana to be a surprise. She hoped he wanted her here. They'd only had a week together, but their connection felt like it had been much longer. The next day would have to be soon enough to see her friends.

Full of pizza and hope for the future, she picked up her phone and selected Mark's number.

"Mrs. Lewis, welcome back to The Plaza. I hope you enjoy your stay." The bellhop placed her bags near the wardrobe. *"Do you wish for one of the staff to unpack for you?"*

God, how she hated the name Lewis. Bitter about her philandering husband, she'd stayed as far away from him as possible. She'd done her duty and given the man a daughter, and it wasn't her fault he'd fallen from his horse in a drunken stupor and broken his neck. Now she was free to do as she pleased as long as she was discreet. Her daughter slept in the nanny's arms as she ushered the bellhop out of the room.

Once the baby was safely in her bed with the nanny nearby, she was free to explore the city. She stepped out onto the street. As always, she was surprised by the speed at which everything moved. After the slow pace of life on her husband's plantation, city life was much more vibrant and alive. The first years of her marriage had been lonely as her husband fought for the Confederacy. Once the war was over, he'd come home and they'd settled into married life. She tolerated his touch, thankful when she realized she was expecting. He'd been disappointed the baby was a girl, but died before he could impregnate her again. Now she was free. Free of his touch and free to do as she pleased.

She stopped and stared at the back of a Union officer, its familiar blue reminding her of his eyes. It had been over five years, but the sight of a Union officer always made her heart race. Could it be him? Had he made it through the war? Then the anger rose within her. How dare he leave her. He was supposed to fight for her and their love.

She was...

Bette sat up in bed, her mind whirling with questions. Was it him?

Had Elizabeth gotten a chance to see her soldier after the war? Squinting at the sun's blinding rays, she regretted not closing the drapes the night before.

Stumbling to the shower, thoughts of seeing Mark pushed remnants of her dream away. The dreams had stopped after she'd returned to Denver, but they were back her first night in Indiana. The hot water woke her completely, and she hummed along with the song on the radio as she made up her face, memories of Mark on her mind.

She was relieved to see Mark's car parked in its usual spot by the porch. Pulling up next to it, she hoped he hadn't heard her drive up. His car was bigger than hers, effectively hiding it from him. She'd almost told him she was back the night before as they talked on the phone, one of their rambling, three-hour conversations when neither of them wanted to say goodbye. Sneaking onto the porch, she sat in one of the rocking chairs and pulled out her phone. Her fingers flying over the screen she sent a text.

Bette: Good morning

Mark: Morning, beautiful

Bette: Had your coffee?

She knew he liked to sit on the porch and drink his coffee on his days off. Crossing her fingers, she watched the screen.

Mark: Heading that way. Slept in, up too late talking to you.

She watched as the screen door opened, it's distinctive screech covering the sound of her giggle. Mark stood at the stairs and stared out across the field that was his front yard, phone in his left hand, coffee mug in his right. Even in baggy sweats and a t-shirt, he was handsome. Sipping at his coffee, he stretched and yawned.

She hit send on one last text and watched him bring the phone up to read it.

Turn around

He turned and caught sight of her. Forgetting he was holding a mug filled with hot coffee, it sagged and spilled onto his foot. He jumped back. "Shit," he muttered as he set the mug on the table. "What... How... When did you get here?" he grumped.

Knowing he wasn't fully functional until he'd had a least one cup of coffee, she giggled. "I wanted to surprise you."

"You should have..." he started and then stopped. A smile spread across his face. "You're really here." He took her hand, pulled her up out of the chair, and drew her into his arms. "I missed you." She held on as he buried his nose in her hair. "God, I didn't realize just how much until this moment."

She hugged him close, relishing the feel of his arms around her. "Good, 'cause I'm here to stay."

"What?" he asked as he picked up the mug and took a gulp of coffee. "To stay? You moved here?"

"Yeah. Wanna help me unload the U-Haul after I sign the rental agreement for my house?"

"Sure, but first I need more coffee." He moved to the door. "Don't go anywhere. I'll take you to breakfast, and then you've got me for the whole day."

She smiled. "Sounds good, I'm starving. And would you bring me some of that coffee?"

She leaned back in the chair as the screen door slammed behind him. *He'll get tired of you.* She ignored the voice in her head, vowing that "take each day as it comes" would be her new mantra. She smiled when he returned and handed her a mug. Sipping the brew, she smiled. He remembered how she took her coffee, a bit sweet with plenty of creamer. He pulled his chair next to hers and sat, reaching over to take her hand.

After a stop for breakfast and a quick visit to the bookstore to chat with Cassie, they headed to Fort Wayne to get the keys to her rental house and unpack the U-Haul so she could return it.

Mark strode up the porch steps and into the house, setting the box in his hands onto the table. "This one has a shipping label. Where do you want it?"

"I forgot about that one. That one's full of the stuff the nursing home sent after my grandmother passed away. I guess I really should go through it." She picked it up and carried it into the spare room, setting it next to the boxes of items for her store."

She walked back into the living room and found Mark with another box in his hands. "This is the last one. How about we take a break and then turn in the truck?"

Winding her way through the maze of boxes, she went to the kitchen and grabbed two bottles of water from the counter. "I'd offer to cook you dinner, but that would require a trip to the grocery and I'm tired. Rain check?"

"Sure. Why don't we order a pizza and work on at least getting the boxes cleared out of the living room?"

By the time the pizza arrived, they had half of the boxes moved to the appropriate rooms and stacked so she could get to what she needed first.

As Mark paid for the pizza, Bette plopped down on the couch and blew out a breath. "Remind me of this the next time I think it's a good idea to move. Seriously, I'm wiped out."

"Hey, how about some help here?" Mark asked, looking down at her.

She jumped up and took the bottles of soda so he could set the pizza box on the table. Flipping up the lid, he pulled out a slice and sat on the couch.

Bette watched as he chewed, wondering how she'd gotten so lucky to find such a good friend. She opened one of the sodas and took a sip, remembering how they met. The chaos of the accident scene and him being the one to treat her injuries seemed both like yesterday and long ago. She'd been grateful for his care, but now there was something else between them, a feeling she was afraid to name. If she acknowledged it, how would she deal if he didn't feel the same? What if he only wanted to be friends? Pushing the thought away, she replaced it with an image of him moving in closer until his lips met hers.

"I thought you were hungry. You okay?" He sat forward, his eyes looking over her face.

"Oh, yeah. I was just remembering how we met." She didn't want to tell him where her thoughts had taken her.

"You better grab some of this pizza. I may eat it all if you don't." He reached out and snagged another slice.

Picking up a slice, she bit into it and moaned. It was the perfect temperature, the cheese still gooey but not so hot it burned the roof of her mouth.

Mark laughed as she took another huge bite and smiled at him.

Her attention on the pizza, she didn't notice him staring while she chewed.

He reached over and wiped a glob of sauce off her lip, his eyes following his thumb.

She stared as he licked the sauce off, her tongue caressing the spot where it had been.

"Damn," he whispered and then swallowed hard. "I, uh, I... Oh, to hell with it." He reached over, wrapped his hand around the back of her neck, and pulled her closer to him until his lips met hers.

With a sigh, she opened her mouth and let him deepen the kiss, moaning at the fire racing through her veins. Her hands roamed, moving under the bottom of his shirt to splay against the warm skin of his back. Never had a mere kiss sparked such an intense response.

He pulled away, panting. "I'm not sorry."

"What?" she breathed as she blinked at him. "Why would you be sorry?"

"I just...watching your lips, I couldn't stop myself. I mean, I usually ask someone out on a date before I kiss them."

With a smile, she tugged him closer, bringing her lips up to his ear to whisper, "I wasn't complaining."

"I was afraid you weren't into me as more than a friend."

With a snort, she laughed louder. "Hey, I moved all the way from Denver to Indiana to be closer to you." She put her hand over her mouth, but it was too late. The truth had already slipped out. "I didn't mean to say that."

He sighed and brushed at the hair hanging in her face, tucking it behind her ear. "I'm glad you did. I've been debating all day whether or not to say what was on my mind." He took her hand and pulled her closer to him, fitting his hips to hers. "And by the way, those jeans should be illegal. When we dropped off the truck, I thought I'd have to punch the clerk 'cause of the way he was ogling you."

"No, he wasn't," she exclaimed with a blush. She twisted and brushed at the seat of her jeans, thinking maybe she'd sat in something. "I'm sure you're mistaken."

"When you bent over to pick up the pen you dropped, I thought his eyes were going to bug out of his head." He pulled her closer and whispered in her ear. "I wanted to pick you up, carry you out of the store, and find the nearest horizontal surface so I could…" his voice dropped off to a whisper, "ravish you."

"There's a couch right here," she whispered back. "Have at it."

His eyes darkened, the pupils almost blocking out the blue. After yanking his shirt over his head, he picked her up and laid her on the couch, following her down.

All of his weight on his arms, he looked down at her. "Are you sure?"

She couldn't believe he had to ask. "Yes, I'm sure," she said as she cupped the back of his neck with her hand. A slight tug and he dropped to his elbows. "It's just… God, this is awkward." He dropped his head so she couldn't see his face.

"What? Talk to me."

"I feel like this is going too fast, that something I didn't think of will go wrong and ruin—"

"Look at me."

He brought his head up, concern and uncertainty written in his eyes.

"We don't have to…"

"I want to. I just…it's been…I normally don't…" He closed his eyes and took a deep breath. "The thing is, I don't have a lot of experience at this whole relationship thing." He lowered his head again, "or with being…intimate."

Her eyes widened. "Are you telling me you're a…"

He laughed and kissed her. "No, but I've only been with a couple of women, and I don't want to disappoint you."

Reaching up, she cupped his jaw. "We don't have to do this tonight if you're feeling unsure." She kissed him.

He groaned and deepened the kiss. "Don't even joke about that. This feels different." He went on at her frown, "Good different, like it means something more."

Bette opened her eyes and cuddled into the heat at her back.

Mark groaned. "You know what that does to me, right?" He jerked when the alarm on his phone blared. "Shit, I'm gonna be late." He jumped up and pulled on his jeans. "I don't want to leave but I've got a shift in…" he checked his phone, "twenty minutes. If I leave right now, I might make it."

Tugging on her clothes, she started toward the kitchen. "Give me five minutes to make you some coffee."

"No time." He ran his fingers down her arm. "This isn't how I wanted our first morning to go." He kissed her quickly and stepped back. "If I don't leave now I won't leave at all." He picked his keys up from the coffee table as he shoved his phone in his pocket. "I'll call you later."

She watched as he hurried out the door, smiling at his sleep-tousled hair. The nurses were going to have a field day with that. She stretched, loving the slight soreness from their overnight activities. Who would have thought her not-very-experienced doctor was a very quick study. With a yawn, she shuffled to the kitchen to make herself some coffee. All those boxes weren't going to unpack themselves, but first she needed to assemble the shelves.

The doorbell rang as she struggled to hold the pieces of the rack together while she pounded in the bolt. Wiping sweat off her forehead, she opened the door and smiled. Cassie and Ragan stood on her porch with a bag from a local restaurant.

"Mark sent you lunch, and reinforcements," Cassie said with a smile.

"Awesome, come on in."

Ragan went to the kitchen for plates and silverware while Cassie put the bag of food on the dining room table, reaching in to pull out to-go containers.

Bette grabbed the one with her name on it, sniffing as she opened it. "Oooh, General Tso's Chicken, my favorite!"

Containers in hand, they sat and ate as they discussed what Bette still needed to accomplish.

"The biggest thing is getting those stupid shelves put together. I was having problems holding the pieces together so I could get the bolts put in."

"I'm not mechanically inclined but I'm really good at holding things," Cassie said as she forked up another bite of shrimp fried rice. "I tried to put together an entertainment center once. It wasn't pretty."

They laughed as they carried their empty containers to the kitchen. "Just put them on the counter, I'll take care of them later when I find the garbage bags."

Cassie opened the dishwasher. "Go get started, I'll get these dishes unpacked and loaded in the dishwasher."

"Thanks, Cassie," Bette said as she turned to head for the bedroom she was using as the base of her business. "You two showing up was just what I needed. Those shelves were driving me crazy."

Ragan chuckled as she picked up the instructions. "Let's see what's what." After studying the paper, she picked up one of the shelves and handed it to Bette. "Hold this here," she pointed as she picked up a bolt and nut. As she screwed on the nut she asked, "So, you and Mark seem to be getting along…" Her voice trailed off.

"Yeah. We just seemed to click. I mean, how weird is it that I was ready to move eleven hundred miles to be near him after only a week?"

"I get it. When I met Adam, the attraction was immediate and really intense."

"Is Adam why you broke it off with Mark?" Flexing her fingers, Bette waited for Ragan to continue.

"Well, yes, but it wasn't that simple." Ragan explained that she'd been unaware she was pregnant when she'd broken things off with Adam after her stalker threatened him, leaving Fairfield Corners without a goodbye. Running away to the Congo, she met a handsome English doctor and tried to move past her love for Adam Bricklin. "When I came back to town, I had no idea Adam had moved here. Thanks to a sudden snowstorm, I crashed my car and ended up in the river. Thank God Adam saw it happen or we might not have survived."

"Oh, wow," Bette exclaimed. "How did Mark fit into all of this?"

"Well, I was still scared my stalker would hurt Adam, so I started dating Mark. We've known each other since we were kids and there was a spark there, but fate had other ideas." She put down the allen wrench she was using to tighten the nuts and turned to face Bette. "There's something you need to know before I continue this story."

They both turned when Cassie walked into the room, followed by another woman. "More reinforcements have arrived."

Ragan smiled. "Bette, this is my sister-in-law, Faith."

"I was just telling Bette how I ended up married to Adam."

Faith smiled, "I never get tired of hearing this story. Gets my writer brain churning."

Ragan laughed. "Just to warn you, anything you say could end up in a book. Faith writes the most amazing romance novels."

"Now, don't scare her, Ragan."

"Oh hush," Faith laughed. "Now, finish the story."

"Okay, okay. I was just going to explain to Bette how I have visions."

"Visions? What kind of visions?" Bette asked.

"Of the future, though they may only be a few minutes into the future." She took a sip of water from the bottle Cassie handed her. "So, not long after I came back to town, Adam got drunk and wound up at my house. We ended up making love, but he thought it was something nonconsensual. Anyway, I was having visions of a person writing notes about someone dying and knew it was my stalker writing about Adam."

Bette stared at her. "So, were did Mark fit into all this?"

"I knew I still loved Adam, but I also had feelings for Mark. I was convinced my stalker would hurt or maybe even kill Adam, so I stayed with Mark until I discovered I was pregnant with Adam's baby."

"Then what happened? How did you end up with Adam?"

"Well, I refused to allow a stalker to keep Adam from knowing this child, so I broke it off with Mark. Adam and I were finally working things out between us when I was kidnapped by my stalker. Turns out, my stalker was Mark's younger brother, Billy, who'd been obsessed with me for years."

Bette paled. "He's the one who died in the room upstairs?"

"Yes." Ragan brushed at a tear. "No one knew how bad his psychosis had gotten. He tried to shoot Adam, but the Fairfield ghost saved him, killing Billy instead."

"No wonder Mark keeps that room locked."

"Time to change the subject. I hate talking about that without a glass of wine. That reminds me, Cassie has book club this Thursday night. Be at the bookstore at seven."

Bette grinned. "But I haven't read the book."

"Doesn't matter. Our group is called Words and Wine, and we want you to be there. Now, put on some music and let's get these shelves up."

Chapter Eleven

BETTE CHECKED her website and grinned at the orders. At this rate, she'd need to find a store sooner than she'd thought. Placing the last couple of items on a shelf, she cut down the box and added it to the pile. One box left and she'd be done.

Noting the shipping label, she realized it contained her grandmother's things sent to her by the nursing home. She brushed away a tear, saddened by the thought that her grandmother's life had been condensed into one small box. She'd pushed it into the corner and tried to forget about it. She set the box in front of her on the packing table and cut through the tape, pulling the flaps back.

On top, wrapped in bubble wrap, was her grandmother's favorite picture. Her mother and grandmother on either side of her, Bette was blowing out the candles on a birthday cake, her cheeks puffed out like a chipmunk. Her eighteenth birthday party had been the last time the three of them had been together—two weeks later, her mother died in a car accident. Her grandmother never recovered from the loss of her daughter, and rapidly advancing Alzheimer's finally took her five years later. Bette reverently set the picture aside and pulled out more bubble wrap. Some figurines and a few more pictures, and she then was at the bottom of the box. Pulling out one last sheet of bubble wrap she discovered a couple of old books. An old leather-bound journal and an even older book under a sheet of notebook paper. She recognized her grandmother's handwriting.

This was my grandmother's journal. I hope you find it helpful.

Setting the paper down, she picked up the journal, its leather cover brittle and cracking.

Carefully, she opened the cover. Written in perfectly shaped letters was the name Elizabeth Hamilton. That was too weird. *This can't be the same Elizabeth, can it?*

Inventory and thoughts of a storefront forgotten, she carried the book to the living room, plopped into her favorite chair, and started reading.

Lost in the world of antebellum Georgia, the ringing of her phone startled her, the jarring noise out of place. The phone now silent, she blinked and realized it had been three hours since she discovered the books. She'd been engrossed, reading every entry. Each page pulled her further into the ill-fated story of Lizzie and Marcus. Her great-great grandmother and Mark's great-great grandfather. *I have to tell Mark I found Lizzie.*

The phone buzzed with a text notification, so she reached to pick it up.

Mark: Anna found Lizzie's descendants. Walking out the door now, be there soon.

Well, at least she wouldn't have to wait long to tell him.

A fresh glass of water at her side, she curled up on the couch and opened the book, returning to the page she'd been reading when Mark called.

Lizzie had written of her love for her soldier and how his defection hardened her heart toward him, even though she still loved him fiercely. She wrote how she'd cast a spell that would plague the Fairfield family for generations to come. Fleeting happiness followed by crushing grief and despair. As she'd cast the spell, she wasn't even sure it would work. The book of spells she'd gotten from her mother hadn't contained a spell to do exactly what she'd wanted, so she'd modified one that was close.

Lost in the world of Lizzie and the revelation that she was both a witch and her ancestor, Bette didn't hear Mark unlock the door. His footsteps on the wood floor echoed throughout the room as he strode toward her. She finished the last entry and her mind whirled with questions.

He dropped down onto the couch next to her and reached for the book. "What's this?"

Reverently, she closed the journal. "Lizzie's diary."

"What?"

"It was in the box of my grandmother's things." She turned and looked at him. "Lizzie was my great-great, grandmother."

Shocked, he stared at the book. "You're sure it's the same Lizzie?"

She opened the book and started reading, "I met the most handsome man today. Marcus Fairfield from Indiana. Such a strong name and so handsome. He's a Union soldier, so I don't know how Father will react." She closed the book and handed it to him.

"Maybe now Marcus can rest in peace."

He'll leave now that he has no more reason to be with you. She closed her eyes and breathed deeply, willing the thoughts out of her head. The last line she'd read echoed in her mind,

I've cast the spell that will bind my spirit to my descendants. I will have an eternity to search for my soldier and exact justice.

Was it Lizzie's spirit putting those awful thoughts in her head? Thoughts of betrayal and heartache. Or was she imagining it?

Pushing thoughts of Lizzie and the journal to the back of her mind, she looked at Mark and smiled. "Hey, handsome. You hungry?" She stood and plucked the journal out of his hand. "I've got a pork roast in the slow cooker, and it should be about ready. Wait until you taste my pulled pork."

"You trying to change the subject?" He reached for the book. "What else does it say?"

"I haven't read it all yet." She didn't want to tell him that Lizzie thought she was a witch. That was crazy, right?

She opened the lid of the slow cooker, and the tangy scent of cooked pork filled the kitchen. Poking at the meat with a fork, she determined it was done. Mark's hand covered hers, poked the fork into the roast and twisted to spear some of the meat. She tried to grab the fork, but he held it up over her head, out of her reach. "Hey, give me that."

He put the meat in his mouth and chewed. His stomach gave a loud rumble. "Well, my taste buds enjoyed that, and it sounds like my stomach agrees."

She laughed and turned to face him. "Then I guess I better feed you." After a quick kiss on his lips, she turned back to the counter and turned off the slow cooker. "It needs to cool for about ten minutes so I can pull it." She handed him plates and silverware. "Here, set the table for me? I also made potato salad, it's in the big bowl in the fridge." Grabbing the package of buns, she put it on top of the plates in his hands and then pushed him toward the table. "Don't expect this all the time, these are the two things I can cook well. I'm more of a baker than a chef."

She felt him behind her before his arms came around her. "Hey, I thought you were hungry?" Shredding the pork, she transferred it to the platter. His breath tickled her ear.

"I'm starving," he whispered, biting her earlobe before kissing her neck. Then his heat was gone and he was at the fridge. "But I guess we should eat first. You want a beer or iced tea?"

Her knees weak, she leaned against the counter. "A beer would be great." She turned to the table, the platter of pulled pork in her hands.

The television program faded to the background as she read more entries from Lizzie's journal. Mark's head in her lap, she smiled at his soft snore. She read of forbidden love, clandestine meetings, and plans to run away. The love Lizzie felt for Marcus practically soaked from the pages into her fingertips. In between entries written about love and longing were entries about magic and witchcraft, and how she'd found her mother's Book of Shadows and began experimenting with the spells within it. And then she noticed an abrupt change. In one entry she'd been so in love and looking forward to her life with her soldier, but the next was different. They became filled with loathing for her father and her new husband, but the worst entries depicted an overwhelming hatred for the one she believed betrayed her—Marcus.

Horrified, she continued to read, sucked into the story told by her ancestor. A loveless marriage and unwanted sex, but with one bright spot —her daughter. She would not make the same mistake as her mother. Lizzie vowed to teach her daughter about her power at an early age. No one would take advantage of her daughter the way her father and Marcus had of her.

Chapter Twelve

BETTE COLLAPSED ONTO THE COUCH, watching as Cassie and Ragan did the same, dropping her shopping bags to the floor. Faith lowered herself into a chair with a sigh and kicked off her shoes.

"Why is shopping so fun, yet exhausting?" Bette asked with a groan. "I'm pooped."

They'd spent the afternoon at the open-air mall in Fort Wayne, hitting almost every store before returning to Bette's house to relax and decide what to do about dinner.

"I want to check out your house now that it's put together, but I don't want to move," Cassie griped. "My feet are killing me."

"Anyone else thirsty?" Bette asked as she pushed herself up off the couch. "And I need to know what sushi you want. I'll call in an order for delivery." She opened the drawer in the end-table and pulled out the to-go menu. "What time are the guys supposed to be here?"

"Seven. They wanted to take the kids to the arcade after dinner." Ragan replied.

Cassie pulled out her phone. "I better check in with Logan. Dane is still having a hard time adjusting."

Bette looked up. Dane was Cassie and Logan's foster son. His dad was the one who'd kidnapped Bette in Denver. "Do you think it would help if I talked to him?"

"It might. He feels guilty about what his dad did. Violet is the only one who can get him talk about it. From the first day, Dane and Violet have been inseparable."

"How about tomorrow?"

"That sounds good. Come later in the day and you can stay for dinner."

"Okay. So, who's ready for wine?" Bette asked as she walked into the kitchen, smiling at the yeses coming from her friends.

As she uncorked the wine, Bette felt an itch in her brain, as if someone was brushing it with a feather. She turned, wine glasses in her hands.

Lizzie looked out of eyes that weren't her own and stared at the room around her. She searched Bette's mind, pleased to discover this was a kitchen. Bright and sparkling, she marveled at the lack of a woodstove. Running her hands along the table, she looked at the bottle and was pleased to discover it was wine, though it was a variety she was not familiar with. Pouring a glass she tasted it, enjoying the sweetness.

"Bette, what's taking so long? We need the wine!" Cassie said as she walked into the room.

Lizzie looked her up and down, marveling at a female wearing trousers. "Who are you?"

"What do you mean? It's me, Cassie." She peered at her friend. "You okay, Bette?"

"I'm not Bette, I'm Lizzie." She sipped at her wine. "Tell me, what year is it?"

Cassie pulled her phone out of her pocket and scrolled to find Mark's number. "Hey, Ragan, can you come here?" She said loudly as the phone rang.

"Hello. Cassie?" she heard Mark ask as Ragan joined her in the kitchen.

"Oooh, Moscato." She reached for the bottle and one of the empty glasses on the table.

"Bette isn't quite…herself," Cassie said into her phone.

"What do you mean?" she heard from both Mark and Ragan.

Her eyes on Ragan she replied to Mark, "She says her name is Lizzie."

Faith stood in the doorway, staring as a blurry version of someone's face superimposed itself over Bette's. *What in the world?*

Lizzie twirled the glass in her hand, watching the yellowish liquid run up and then down the sides in a wave. "Is this all you do?" she asked, her boredom plain on her face. "I guess it's better than working all day." Sipping the wine, she held out the glass with a frown. "More, please."

Ragan jumped up when she heard the front door open. "Mark's here," she said as she raced toward the living room.

"Where is she?" Mark questioned as he scanned the room. "What happened?"

Her hand on his arm, Ragan pulled him back. "Bette went to the kitchen to open the wine and suddenly she changed. Said she was Lizzie and asked what year it was."

Mark sat, "Shit, it's true."

Ragan crouched in front of him. "What's true? What's going on?"

"I knew I'd find you."

Mark looked past Ragan and found Bette watching him, but it wasn't the woman he knew. Something about her face was different...*her eyes*. They were the same deep brown, but they practically glittered with hatred.

He swallowed as his mind raced. Give him a difficult injury or illness and he knew what to do. His girlfriend possessed by her pissed-off ancestor? No clue how to handle that. "Lizzie?"

"You favor him, with your good looks and kind eyes. Tell me, are you as skilled at lying as he was?" She walked closer and purred, "I'm going to enjoy making you suffer."

"Suffer? Why? How?"

"I'm not sure yet. Maybe you'll suffer an early death. Or, even better, this Bette that you seem to be enamored with." She sipped at the wine. "Or maybe something job related." She paused as she searched Bette's memories. "You're a physician. How about I kill one of your patients?"

He stepped back, his horror at the thought written across his face. "No, please, not a patient."

"Oooh, I struck a nerve. Interesting."

He stepped back toward her. "No. I won't let you terrorize me."

Suddenly sagging against the table, the wine glass dropped out of her hand and shattered on the ceramic tile.

Mark caught her before she could hit the floor.

"Bette? Open your eyes, beautiful."

She blinked up at him. "What? Mark? When did you get here?"

He lowered her onto the couch, his hand gentle as he brushed at the hair on her forehead to get a clear look into her eyes. "You don't remember?"

Crouched next to her, he looked up at Ragan. "My bag is in the car. Get it for me?"

Ragan hurried off and Cassie took her place at the back of the couch. "Is she okay?" Her face pale, she rubbed her arms.

"Cassie, go sit. You look almost as pale as Bette."

"This just hits a little close to home. Brought back a few unpleasant memories." She dropped into the chair and sighed.

"Yeah, well, it scared the crap out of me."

"What happened?" Bette asked, her eyes wide. "What scared you?"

"You had an episode of some sort. Claimed you were Lizzie." He held her wrist and frowned as her pulse increased.

"An episode?" Her breathing quickened as she tried to make sense of what Mark was telling her. "I said I was Lizzie?" She remembered the passage she'd read about a binding spell. *Is it true? Is my great grand-mother bound to me?*

"Hey, relax. Everything's fine."

"No, I can't relax." She sat up and gazed around the room. "Did I do anything else?"

Cassie perched on the edge of the chair. "No, you sipped your wine and talked. That's it."

She poked at the dark spot in her memory, puzzled at the blankness. It wasn't that she couldn't remember, it was as if she had been some-where else. She had a vague sense of nothingness. Poking at the blank spot made her nauseous, but she couldn't seem to stop. "Why can't I remember?" she muttered.

Mark frowned as her face paled. "Hey, it's okay. Lie back and relax."

Disliking the nausea, she complied, hoping it would help.

Mark looked up as the door slammed and Ragan hurried over with his bag, Logan in step behind her.

Mark opened his bag and pulled out the blood pressure cuff, visibly more relaxed now that he could do something. He looked over at Cassie, glad to see Logan by her side. His attention back on Bette, he smiled at her blood pressure and checked her pulse again.

Ragan handed him a blanket. "Thanks," he said as he unfolded it and covered Bette up to her chin. "Now, lie here and relax. You still look shaken."

He stood and motioned for Cassie to follow him to the kitchen. "Now, are you okay?"

"Yeah, it just brought up some scary memories." She shuddered. "More importantly, is Bette okay?"

"I think so. I'm hoping I'll be able to convince her to get a cat scan. The memory loss is troubling." He rubbed his hands over his face. "I'm worried. I watched what my brother went through and..." he swallowed and sighed, "I don't know if I can watch someone else go through that again."

"You really think it's a mental illness? Even after everything Logan and I went through?"

"I want to believe it, but..."

Ragan walked into the room and interrupted him. "You've known for years that I have visions. Why is it so hard to believe in witchcraft or reincarnation?"

He sat at the table and ran his hands through his hair. "I don't know. I've got these feelings for Bette, strong feelings, and I'm just afraid."

"Afraid? Why?" Cassie asked as she pulled a chair nearer to him and sat.

"Afraid because, deep down, I do believe. And if I believe in those things, I also have to believe in the curse on my family. The curse of fleeting happiness."

"Hey, it's going to be okay." Cassie pulled him closer for a hug.

"I hope you're right."

"I am. Now, we need to learn all we can about what's happening to Bette. You said this Lizzie was a witch?"

"Yeah, a natural witch, whatever that means." He rubbed his eyes leaned back in his chair. "I'll do whatever it takes to help Bette."

Ragan placed a cup of coffee in front of him. "Here, you look like you could use something warm."

He looked up at Ragan, a lopsided grin on his face. "Did I ever tell you I'm glad you found Adam? I know I thought I was in love with you and…"

"Shhh…," she interrupted him as she sat on the other side of him. "We weren't meant to be, that's all." Picking up his hand, she continued, "You belong with Bette, anyone can see it when you two are together."

"But how can we help her? Something medical I can deal with, but this…" He stopped and swallowed. "This is something I can't control."

Ragan hugged him and then stood when they heard a car pull up into the drive. "Adam is here with the kids."

Cassie picked up the untouched cup of coffee and carried it to the sink. "I might know someone who can help. There's a coven in Fort Wayne."

"A coven? You mean witches? Do I want to know how you know that?" Mark stood and paced to the doorway. "I…I'll do anything to help her."

"They're normal people who happen to have a talent or interest in magic. I talked to the coven leader when I was doing research during my demon issue." She dumped the coffee and swished clean water in the cup. "I'll text you her name and number."

Ragan stepped into Adam's embrace when he walked into the room, AJ on his hip. "Hey, beautiful," he said as he kissed her temple. "Everything okay?"

"Not really. I'll explain on the drive home." She held out her hands to AJ who giggled and shook his head. "Seriously? You are such a daddy's boy." She turned and looked at Mark. "Call me if you need anything."

"Sure," he mumbled as he crouched next to Bette and took her hand in his."

"Hey, you okay?" Robbie asked as Faith rubbed her hands up and down her arms, as if she was cold.

"Yeah." She sat next to him on the couch and curled her feet up under her. "I just…I saw something weird when Bette was having her episode today."

He draped his arm over her shoulders and pulled her close, tucking her head under his chin. "What did you see?"

"It looked like there was a ghost's face superimposed over Bette's. It was similar to hers, but not quite the same."

"You think it was a ghost? The ghost of her great grandmother?" He laced his fingers in with hers.

"Yeah," she said with a sigh. "I guess I can see any ghost and not just my grandmother."

"We need to tell Mark. Maybe it will convince him it's not something that can be explained medically."

She sighed and looked up at him. "You're right, as usual. I was hoping we could keep my gift a secret, but he needs to know."

Chapter Thirteen

BETTE SAT in her car in front of Cassie's house and watched Dane and Violet. Heads bent over a comic book, Dane's dark hair was in stark contrast to Violet's fiery red. Laughing and gesturing at the page, they didn't notice her staring at them. At least something good had come from the terrible situation—Cassie and Logan had been approved as Dane's foster parents.

With a sigh, she got out of the car and ambled up the sidewalk, not wanting to see the smile leave his face when he realized who she was. According to Cassie, his smiles were few and far between. Stopping at the bottom of the stairs she cleared her throat and said, "Hi, Dane."

He stood and placed himself in front of Violet, as if to protect her. "What do you want?" He scanned the street behind her and looked toward the house next door. "Vi, go get your mom."

"I didn't mean to scare you. You probably don't recognize me." She fidgeted with the strap of her purse. "Your dad took…"

He studied her face. "You're the woman from the camper. My dad kidnapped you."

"Yes, he did. But he didn't hurt me."

"What do you want?"

"I was hoping we could talk."

He looked back at the screech and subsequent slam of the screen door.

Violet, her hand in Cassie's, looked scared.

"It's okay Dane, I asked Bette to come talk to you today," Cassie said, her hand holding Vi's.

His shoulders relaxed but his eyes remained wary, watching her as she climbed the steps.

Cassie picked up Violet and turned to Dane. "Why don't I get you some Kool-Aid and you can have a talk with Bette."

She led them back to the kitchen and motioned to the table.

"You want some coffee, Bette?"

"That would be nice. Just a bit of sugar and plenty of creamer."

Bette watched as she busied herself pouring coffee and Kool-Aid.

"If you need more, just help yourself."

"Thanks Cassie. This is perfect." Bette said after taking a sip of the beverage.

"Come on, Vivi," Cassie said as she held out her hand. "Let's go and watch your mermaid movie." She looked over at Bette. "Find me when you're done here."

"Okay."

Once they were gone, Bette wrapped her hands around the mug. "Cassie told me you're having a hard time adjusting."

He nodded and stared at the glass of Kool-Aid in front of him. "She's nice but I miss my dad."

"I understand. I'm sure Cassie talked to you about why he's in the hospital."

"Yeah, we went to see him the other day. He looks better."

"I'm glad." And she was. Cassie had explained how he'd had a mental break after the death of his wife and was now being treated. "I want you to know I hope he gets better."

"He still might go to jail, even though he was sick, and that's why he did that to you," Dane stated sadly.

"What he did was scary, but I forgive him. And I want you to understand that there was nothing you could have done to stop it."

He hung his head. "Cassie told me that too."

"Well, she's right." She sipped at her coffee.

"I feel guilty that you got hurt. If it wasn't for me, he…"

"It wasn't your fault. I think something broke inside him when your mom died, something that you couldn't see."

The haunted look in his eyes tore at her heart.

"But I did see. I could see that he was different. If I'd told someone, maybe you wouldn't have gotten hurt."

Bette scooted her chair closer to Dane's so they were face to face. Taking his hands in hers she said, "Oh, Dane, you have to stop blaming yourself. You're just a kid." She brushed the hair off his forehead.

"I'm almost eight," he grumbled.

With a smile she replied, "Oh, my bad. You're practically a grown up."

He smiled and her heart melted. "I want to tell you a secret. Will you promise not to tell?"

He nodded. "Yeah, I'll even pinkie swear."

"I'm glad your dad kidnapped me."

Puzzled, he asked, "Why would that make you happy?"

"Because it brought me here to Fairfield Corners. I don't know if Cassie told you, but I moved here a couple of weeks ago." She leaned back and sipped at her coffee. "I never would have met Mark if your dad hadn't grabbed me."

He jumped up and hugged her. "I was worried that you'd try to have them lock my dad up for a long time."

Cassie poked her head into the kitchen. "Everything okay in here?" Her eyes widened at the sight of Dane hugging Bette.

"Yeah, I think things will be better now."

"Good. Now, who wants cookies?"

Dane sat back in his chair and wiped the tears off his face. "I do."

Cassie pulled four cookies out of the jar on the counter and handed them to the boy. "Two for you and two for Vivi."

He ran out of the room.

"That poor kid," Bette said. "He was afraid I was going to have them put his dad in prison forever or something. He's had so much sorrow in his life already."

"We've been taking him to a therapist, but I think your talk today did a lot of good. His eyes look happier."

"I'm glad." She fiddled with the cup in front of her. "Have you decided what you're going to do with the empty store in your building?"

"No, I thought about expanding but I really don't have a reason to do that." She got the coffeepot and poured more coffee into Bette's mug.

"Well…" Bette stood and went to stare out the window. "Bette's Beautiful Things has been doing well online and I think I'm ready to start looking for a space.

"You should come down tomorrow and check out the store. See if it's what you had in mind." She returned the pot to the coffeemaker. "I love the stuff you sell. We could do promos and…" she clapped her hands, "If I knock out that wall between the two spaces people could browse while waiting for their coffee."

Two hours later Cassie hugged Bette before shooing her out the door. She would be back to Fairfield Corners the next day to check out the space. Bette drove toward Mark's house, itching to tell him her good news.

Chapter Fourteen

BETTE CHECKED her reflection in the mirror again, nerves making her stomach flip. Mark seemed happy to have her back in Indiana but Lizzie's voice in her head had her doubting the move was the right thing to do. He'd seemed excited when she'd told him she was looking at the store in Cassie's building as a possible space for her business, but she was still worried. She turned when she heard the doorbell. "Stay out of my head tonight, please," she muttered as she opened the door. It was their first actual date, dinner at an upscale Mexican restaurant.

Mark stood on her porch, sunglasses in his hand. He looked her up and down. "Wow," he whispered.

Her cheeks pinked as she returned his stare, glad she'd chosen her favorite wrap dress as it was snug in all the right places. Mark looked dashing in slacks and a suit jacket. "Hey, handsome, you look pretty good yourself."

Her hand in his, he led her to his car and opened the door for her, waiting until she was settled to close the door and jog around to the driver's side. He slid in and stared at her again. "How did I get so lucky?"

"You? You saved me from being hurt worse if they'd righted that truck with me still in the back. I'm the lucky one."

He kissed her knuckles and then put the car in gear.

At the restaurant, he placed his hand at the small of her back as they walked in the door. Once they were seated by the hostess, she looked around the room. Cloth tablecloths and muted music let her know this wasn't your run-of-the-mill Mexican restaurant. "This is a nice place. Have you been here before?"

"Yeah, Ragan and I…" he started and then stopped. "Sorry."

"Don't worry, Ragan told me the whole story, you don't have to apologize."

"Anyway, they have some good top-shelf tequilas."

She studied the menu, trying to narrow down her choice when their waiter introduced himself and told them the specials. "I think I'll try the jalapeno margarita."

Mark ordered a beer and the waiter hurried away. "So, are you up to try the dinner for two?"

"That sounds good." She sipped at her water, wondering how to get her date to relax. "So, Ragan told me about your brother. I'm so sorry."

The waiter returned with their drinks and Mark ordered their meal.

"I understand if you don't want to talk about it." She sipped her drink, her eyes widening with delight. "Oh my, this is so good."

"That's why I ordered a beer, the margaritas go down really easy."

"I believe you." She sipped at her drink. "How was your day?"

Mark was telling her a story about a patient when she felt Lizzie push her way forward. Taking a sip of the margarita she smacked her lips. "What in the world is this drink? It is delicious."

Mark stared at her. "What do you mean? You know that's a margarita."

"I'm sure your Bette knows what it is, but I do not."

"Lizzie?"

"Well, of course. Who else would it be?"

Mark scanned the restaurant, no one was paying any attention to their odd conversation. "What do you want? Let me talk to Bette."

"Oh, relax. I'm not going to hurt your precious Bette. I was bored hanging out in her mind. All she thinks about is you and her business. I think you'd be happy to discuss something else."

"Did you really put a curse on my family?"

"Well, yes. Marcus betrayed me; he didn't deserve to be happy."

"What about the rest of my family? They didn't do anything to you. Did they deserve what your curse did to them?"

"That's none of my concern. Now, what type of restaurant is this?"

"Mexican," he said, exasperated. "How can you not care what your curse did to my family?"

"As long as Marcus was punished, I'm happy." She clapped her hands when the waiter returned with two plates piled with food. She sniffed the aromas and sighed. "I've never had this type of food, but it smells divine." She stuck her fork in the beans and took a bite.

Mark sat and stared, unable to take his eyes off the woman sitting across from him. She looked like his Bette, but he knew it wasn't. "Please, let me talk to Bette," he hissed.

She took another bite, this one of the smothered burrito, smiling as she chewed. She frowned when he motioned to the waiter.

"Can I get the bill please?"

"Is everything okay with your meal, sir?"

"Yes, we just need to leave."

"Let me at least get your dinner boxed up for you." He picked up both plates and hurried back to the kitchen, returning with to-go boxes full of food.

Lizzie frowned at Mark. "Surely you could have let me finish my dinner."

"No," he growled. "I don't think so. Now, let's go." He pulled out her chair and took her hand, forcing her to follow him out of the restaurant.

Once she was in the car, he buckled her seatbelt before stomping to the driver's side and sliding in. "Why did you do that?"

"Do what?" she asked sweetly.

"Ruin our date." The tires chirped as he raced out of the parking lot. "You must be aware of what's going on around you even if Bette is in control."

"Somewhat. Your Bette was looking forward to your 'date night' so I decided I wanted to experience it."

He sighed and pulled into Bette's driveway, finally able to turn and look at his passenger.

"What are we doing back here? What happened?" Bette asked as she brought her hand up to her head. "What the heck did they put in that drink?"

"Let's get you in the house."

Lifting her out of the car, he carried her to the front door, her head resting on his shoulder.

After unlocking the door, he stepped into the house.

"Where did you get a key?" she asked, her eyes squinted against the light of the lamp.

"I made a copy while we were at the hardware store the other day."

"Okay, good," she mumbled.

"Headache?" he asked as he set her down on the couch.

"Bad one," she said as she rubbed her temple. "Lizzie came back, didn't she?"

"Yes."

"Seriously, that woman needs to go the hell away."

He frowned at her. "How many times has this happened?"

"Just twice. Tonight, and the other day when the girls were here," she replied as she stretched out across the cushions. "It was bad enough when it was just dreams but taking over my life is so much worse." She dropped her head to the cushion, "I just need to rest my eyes for a minute."

Mark draped the afghan over her after removing her shoes. He dropped into the chair across from the couch and watched her sleep. Now that he'd experienced "Lizzie" he knew the situation was getting worse.

The headaches worried him. Were these episodes causing permanent damage? Tomorrow he'd try to convince her to get a CAT scan, the doctor side of him wanted to rule out anything medical even though he knew in his gut they wouldn't find anything. He leaned forward and rubbed his hands over his face. He might as well get comfortable because he wouldn't leave until he knew she was okay.

He laid his coat over the back of the chair, then removed his shoes and belt before lying next to her on the couch. Pulling her close, he buried his nose in her hair with a sigh, willing himself to relax.

He woke to the smell of coffee. Watching Bette walk toward him with a coffee mug in each hand, he asked, "Feeling better?"

She handed him a mug and sat next to him. "I'm sorry Lizzie ruined our first actual date."

He took her hand and pulled her close enough to wrap her in his arms. "It's okay. We'll do it again after we figure this out." She lay her head on his chest, seemingly content to be close to him. "I just wish I knew where to start. Gotta admit, the paranormal is not my strong suit."

"Well, according to her journal, she was convinced she was a witch. And the book we found with the journal does seem to be filled with spells."

"So, do we search the internet for local witches? LocalcovensRUs.com?" He snorted. "Like that's a thing."

"You'd be surprised," she replied as she dug around in her purse for her phone. "Crap, I need to charge this. I'll grab my laptop and we'll start looking."

When Bette left the room, Mark remembered his conversation with Cassie. "Oh wait, Cassie gave me the number of someone in Fort Wayne. I guess they talked to a local coven when she had her demon problem." He still had a hard time believing everything they'd told him about that. He scrolled through his contacts, trying to remember the name Cassie had given him. He'd call them first and then tell Bette. He didn't want to get her hopes up.

Chapter Fifteen

BETTE TOOK a bite of the pastry and moaned, "This should be illegal."

Cassie dropped down onto the couch next to her, coffee and a pastry in her hands. "I know, right?"

"I've got a strange question to ask." Bette set the plate on the table in front of her and wiped her fingers with a napkin. "You told me you did all kinds of research on the paranormal when you had your demon problem. Just saying, I didn't really believe it all until recently."

"I don't blame you. I wouldn't believe it either if it hadn't happened to me." She sipped her coffee. "Now, how can I help?"

"I need to find a witch or a coven. Preferably local." She picked at her fingernails. "We looked online but didn't find anything except generic sites about witchcraft and spells.

"I gave a name to Mark when he asked after the incident in your kitchen. Let's go ahead and give her a call." Phone in hand she stood. "My office is private, so we can make the call there."

Appointment made and address in hand, Bette sent Mark a text: *On my way. See you soon.*

As she drove, she wondered why Mark hadn't mentioned he'd talked to this Lisha about local witches, instead of letting her fruitlessly search the internet.

She was agitated by the time she arrived at Mark's. Storming into the house, she called his name.

Following his voice, she found him in the study, the book of spells open on the desk. "Why didn't you tell me?"

"Tell you what?"

"That Cassie gave you a name of a local witch. You've watched me driving myself nuts trying to get information." She plopped down into the chair in front of the desk. "I mean, I've been searching for two days and you already had a name."

"Christ, I'm sorry. I wanted to talk to Lisha before I told you in case she couldn't help. I only talked to her this morning."

"Well, I've got an appointment with her in an hour. I'm not sure I want you to go with me." She was concerned he was trying to keep things from her. Angry at the tears that welled up at the thought of him keeping secrets from her, she stomped out of the room and into the kitchen.

"Bette, wait," Mark yelled.

Keys in hand, she'd been headed to the door when his shout stopped her in her tracks. *What am I doing?* Taking off before he could explain was something her mother would have done, and she didn't want to be that person.

"Please, don't be mad. I just..." Mark stopped and stared at her, regret plain on his face. "I just wanted to be able to *DO* something. I have no problem handling medical issues, but this? It's crazy how much this whole situation scares me."

His words touched something deep inside of her. "I don't mean to be so bitchy. I think all the stress is getting to me." With a clink, her keys hit the counter and she rushed to him. Throwing her arms around his neck, she pressed her face into his shirt. "I'm sorry."

His arms tight around her, he kissed the top of her head. "I understand, and I'll try to remember you're capable of handling things. I just feel like I have to protect you as much as I can."

Her ear pressed to his chest, she loved the rumble of his words. She lifted her head and looked up at him. "Let's make a promise to each other. No more secrets."

"I can promise that. You?"

"Yes, I promise, too."

Mark stared at the house. wondering about the woman who lived there. It looked so ordinary, not creepy at all. Shaking his head, he mumbled to himself, "This is real life, not a television show." He stood in front of his car and waited for Bette to join him.

"I'm glad she agreed to see us today. I'm ready to get this over with." She tucked the journal and spell book into the crook of her arm, then clasped Mark's hand. "I hope she can help us."

Me too, Bette," he replied before kissing the back of her hand.

She pressed the doorbell, her palm damp from nervousness. "Maybe she…"

The door opened. "You must be Bette. I'm Lisha, please come in."

Bette stared. Lisha was tall, blond, and looked like a fitness instructor, not the head witch of the local coven.

"Something wrong?"

"Oh. No…I…sorry," she stumbled over her words. "But you don't look like a witch."

Lisha smiled. "I get that a lot. We're just normal people who happen to be witches. Some natural, some by choice."

"What do you mean by natural?" Mark asked as they followed their host through the house.

"Natural witches can access the power of the earth without a sacrifice." She led them into a large room full of books, motioning for them to sit on a couch while she leaned against the desk in the center of the room. "I've been doing some preliminary research based on what you told me over the phone." She picked up a folder full of papers. "The Wilding witch line is strong, at least one natural witch in each generation.

"How did I not know this?" Bette asked, her mind whirling with that tidbit of information. "I mean, you think I'd know if my family was magical."

"The last couple of generations tried to distance themselves from their magical ancestry. Your grandmother moved to Colorado to escape persecution in Virginia."

"Oh my."

"Some people can't or won't control their magic. Your mother accidentally set her home on fire, and…well, she spent some time in an institution. The authorities didn't believe her when she told them she was a witch who couldn't control her power."

Her head swam. *My mother was a witch? Is that why she pushed me away? Because she didn't want to hurt me by accident?*

Bette returned her attention back to the conversation when she heard her name. "I'm sorry, what?"

Lisha sat in the chair directly to her right and took her hand. "I know this must be unsettling, but I need you to stay focused. "First off, we need to determine the level of power you have, if any." Lisha stood and pulled Bette up with her. She led her to the open area next to the desk. Holding both of Bette's hands, she closed her eyes and spoke an incantation.

"What was that?" Mark asked from his seat on the couch.

"I cast a circle of protection. This will keep you safe if something happens that I can't control."

Mark stood, his face pale beneath his tan. "What do you mean 'if something happens'?"

Lisha smiled at him. "Magic can be unpredictable, especially with someone untrained. I'm skilled at controlling magic, but there's always a chance that things won't go the way we want."

Pacing the length of the room and back, Mark ranted. "I'm not sure this is a good idea. Isn't there a safer way to do this?

"Mark, please sit. I need to concentrate."

With a frown, Mark returned to the sofa and sat, his posture stiff.

Her attention back on Bette, Lisha gripped her hands tighter. "Now, I need you to open yourself to me when you feel my magic."

"How will I… Oh!" Bette's eyes widened at the sensation of Lisha's magic flowing into her through their entwined hands. "It feels like bubbles fizzing away in my bloodstream."

"Good, now let me tap into your power to see what we're working with." Lisha closed her eyes and murmured another incantation.

Bette's eyelids drooped and she concentrated on the bubbly feeling of Lisha's magic coursing through her. Relaxing into the pleasant sensation, she stiffened when a jolt of what felt like electricity rushed through her. "What *was* that?"

"Shhh…it's okay," Lisha whispered, her brow furrowing in concentration. She dropped Bette's hands when another jolt raced through them. "Okay, that was unexpected." She rubbed her palms against her denim-clad thighs and blew out a breath.

"Unexpected, how?" Bette inquired, her brow furrowed in concern.

"Let's sit." Lisha walked behind the desk and pulled some bottles of water out of a mini-fridge as Bette returned to sit next to Mark on the couch.

"You okay, Bette?" he asked, his eyes searching her face.

"Yeah, that was…interesting."

Lisha handed them both a bottle of water and then took her seat in the chair. "First off, Bette, you are an exceptionally strong natural witch, with a pure, untainted power." She sipped at the water and set the bottle on the table. "But I also felt another source of power."

Bette blinked slowly and Lizzie rushed forward. "You are a strong witch."

"Who am I speaking with?" Lisha asked, her attention focused on Bette whose face now looked thinner and more angular. "Tell me your name."

"You already know who I am. I am the reason these two are here. I am Elizabeth Hamilton, but you may call me Lizzie."

"Why are you here, Lizzie?" Lisha asked.

"I knew the fates would eventually bring me back to my Marcus's family. Now I can feel their suffering, the anguish they deserve for my soldier's abandonment of me."

"But he didn't…" Mark said before Lizzie cut him off.

"I will not listen to your excuses for your ancestor." Lizzie turned her attention back to Lisha. "I know what you want to do, and I refuse to allow it. I shall not be cast out."

Lisha grasped Bette's hands, and a surge of power raced through their connection, pushing Lizzie back to wherever she resided within Bette.

"We'll see about that," Lisha muttered.

Chapter Sixteen

BETTE CONCENTRATED ON THE CANDLE, willing it to light. Chanting the words to the fire spell, she focused her thoughts on the wick, jumping back in surprise when it burst into flame.

"Oh wow," she breathed. Staring at the candle, she didn't notice the floor smoldering under her feet.

She closed her eyes and concentrated on the second and third candles. According to Lisha, lighting two in succession was trickier. Energy swelled around her, and she opened her eyes to see all three candles burning. She clapped her hands, pleased at her accomplishment.

"Bette, what the hell?" Mark yelled as he ran to the sink, spraying water at the floor beneath her chair. Wisps of steam rose around her. He knelt in front of her and removed her right shoe. She was horrified to see it was scorched. He removed the other shoe and inspected both of her feet for burns.

"What?" she asked as she looked down at her feet. "Did I do that?" The floor was charred in a perfect circle around the legs of her chair.

Mark looked up at her, his eyes wide with fear. "I…" he started, swallowing hard and then trying again. "What the hell happened? You told me this would be safe." As he stared at her, she watched as his fear was overtaken by anger. "You could have burned down the house, with us in it!" he yelled as he stood. "This is nuts…you can't— How do I…?" he sputtered.

She stood and grabbed his hand, pulling him closer to her. She brought her hand to his face and cupped his jaw. "I'm okay."

His head dropped forward. "What if I hadn't been here?" He looked up into her eyes. "Promise me you won't do this alone."

"Lisha warned me this might happen. That my magic has been building for years and could quickly overwhelm me." She sank back into the chair. "How do I practice the simplest of spells if I can't control it?" She dropped her head into her hands. "I'll never get Lizzie out of my head."

"We'll figure it out." Staring out the window above the sink, Mark filled a glass from the tap and brought it to her. "Drink this and calm down," he advised. "I'll call Lisha and tell her what happened. There's got to be a way you can do this safely."

She held the glass with both hands to steady it as she sipped at the water. Being in control of her magic was the key to performing the unbinding spell to get Lizzie out of her head. She had to figure this out.

Mark pulled the door closed behind him as he selected Lisha's number. He dropped into the chair on the porch and waited for her to answer, one hand at the back of his neck. His gut churned as he thought about what could have happened if he hadn't walked in when he did. Her freaking shoes had been on fire.

After a quick phone conversation, he'd driven to the house they'd visited a couple of days before. The door opened as he strode up the walkway, Lisha framed in the opening.

"I was afraid something like this would happen," she started.

"A heads up would have been helpful," he growled. "Bette could have burned the house down with her in it."

Lisha ushered him into the house. "She needs to understand the scope of the power available to her so she'll respect her abilities," Lisha explained. "Getting in over her head is the best way to do that. That's why I suggested she practice with another witch. Unfortunately, we're running out of time."

"What do you mean?"

"Bette called me this morning and told me she had another episode. They're coming more frequently, aren't they?"

"She didn't tell me," he mumbled as he rubbed the back of his neck to try and relieve the tension settling there.

"The longer we let this continue, the harder it's going to be to unbind them."

His head dropped. "Shit."

"There is a better solution, but you're not going to like it."

"Tell me," he said as the ache in his gut intensified.

"According to what Bette told me, she didn't have any issues when she was in Denver. The best alternative is for her to leave and practice her magic away from here, away from you, away from Marcus's ghost."

He stared at her, "Is that really the best solution? As much as I hate it, I see the logic."

"There's no way to know how long it will take Bette to become proficient enough to perform the unbinding spell. The coven can do it, but that adds a layer of risk I don't like."

"What risk?"

She sipped her tea and watched him over the rim of her cup. "Severing the connection without Bette's magic makes it more likely the host won't survive."

Mark blanched. "The host? You're telling me unbinding them could kill Bette?"

"Yes."

Mark was numb. After leaving the house, Mark sat in his car and stared at the steering wheel. His gut churned with the knowledge he had to send her away. He would do anything to keep her safe, including living without her.

Chapter Seventeen

LAYING on the bed in the on-call room, Mark stared at his phone, the curser in the texting app blinking as he tried to type out what he knew was best for Bette. Even after all their research into reincarnation and binding spells, they were no closer to figuring out how to stop Lizzie than they were at the beginning. He had discovered that Lizzie came forward more often when they were in his house as the proximity to his grandfather's ghost seemingly gave her more power.

He knew what he had to do. As much as he loved her, he couldn't watch Bette go through that torment again. Each time Lizzie came forward, Bette's pain and confusion increased, lasting longer after each episode. He couldn't put her through any more of it, no matter how he felt about her. He'd finally admitted to himself that he loved Bette. But, as always in his family, his happiness had been fleeting. He had to make her want to go back to Denver.

Mark: *Working late. See you tomorrow?*

Bette: *No, come over after your shift.*

Mark: *Too tired. Maybe tomorrow.*

He wanted nothing more than to spend the night with her, but he knew this was best. Let her think he was losing interest. The phone dinged with another text notification, but he ignored it. Setting his phone to vibrate, he stood and shoved it in the pocket of his lab coat. He had six hours left on his shift and he needed to keep busy, or he'd cave and go to her.

Bette stared at the last text he'd sent. *Maybe tomorrow*. She could feel him pulling away from her. He wasn't taking her calls and his texts had become sporadic. The voice in her head laughed, *I told you he didn't love you.*

"Shut up!" she screamed at the mirror, as if that would stop Lizzie's voice. The episodes were becoming more frequent, and the blinding headaches that came after each one were getting worse. She hoped the coven they'd contacted the week before would quickly come up with a solution. The last one had been so bad it had made her physically ill. Luckily, she'd been home when that one hit. Mark had been at work, so it hadn't been necessary to try and hide the pain from him.

It had been two days since she'd talked to him, either in person or on the phone. They'd talked more often when she'd still been in Denver. Every night, they'd had rambling three-hour conversations before going to sleep. She missed the closeness she'd felt with him. She might be physically close now, but he felt so far away. Selecting his number, she listened to it ring, frowning when his voicemail picked up. "Hey, just wanted to say goodnight. I miss you. I'm going to Evansville tomorrow morning. I'll call you when I get there."

She pulled out her suitcase and began to pack. A buying trip would take her mind off her wayward boyfriend. There were some antique shops down in Evansville she'd been following online that had a couple of items she wanted to see in person. Since it was a five-hour drive, she decided she'd stay the night and head back the next day. Besides, the time alone on the highway would give her the quiet she needed to think about her failing relationship.

Suitcase packed and ready, she went to bed.

Mark stood on his porch, coffee in hand as he stared out across the fields. Storm clouds gathered, matching his mood. Ignoring Bette was tearing at him, wreaking havoc on his sleep. Squinting at the sky, he grimaced at the thumping in his head and the thought of food made him queasy. Slurping more coffee, he turned back to the house and frowned when the lights flickered and then went out. Great. He'd wanted to sand the floor in the kitchen, but no power meant no sanding. He heard his phone ring as he stumbled his way up the stairs. Maybe a hot shower would improve his mood, so whoever it was would just have to wait.

Rubbing his hair with a towel, he returned to the kitchen. The lights flickered on and off and then stayed on, thank God for small favors. He poured some coffee in his mug and stuck it in the microwave to warm it up. As he waited, he checked his phone and found a voice mail from Bette and another from an unknown number. Probably another spam call. As he wasn't up to listening to Bette's voice, he'd drink his coffee first.

His mood improved by the jolt of caffeine, he sat out on his porch and decided it was time to deal with the voicemails. Storm clouds moved eastward, the sun peeking out between them.

The first voicemail was from Bette. "Hey, I think we need to talk. I'm headed out the door, so I'll call when I get to Evansville. Love you."

Those two soft words at the end gutted him. He hated how lost she sounded.

With a sigh, he saved the voicemail and was in the process of pulling up the second when his phone rang. Whoever it was had already left a message, so he answered.

"Hello?"

"Is this Mark Fairfield?"

"Yes, who is this?"

"This is Angela Winfield, I'm a nurse at Fort Wayne Memorial Hospital. I'm calling on behalf of Bette Watson."

His breath caught. "Bette?" Why would a Fort Wayne hospital be… Shit. She was driving to Evansville. "Is she okay?" he asked as he ran to the stairs.

"Ms. Watson was in a traffic accident about thirty minutes ago. She sustained a head injury but is alert and talking. She's being…"

He interrupted her, "I'm a doctor, so don't sugarcoat it. What's her condition?" He stopped and waited for her to answer.

"I don't know, she's still being evaluated."

"I'll be there in twenty minutes."

He shoved his feet into his running shoes and sprinted down the stairs, grabbing his keys off the hook beside the door. With a roar, he sped down the drive, tapping the steering wheel in frustration as he waited for a car to pass so he could hit the road. Driving faster than was safe, his heart thumped in his chest. What if she was badly hurt? Or worse... He swallowed the acid that crept up his throat. *She has to be okay, she just has to be.*

Pulling into the first available parking space, he beeped the locks as he ran toward the ER door. The waiting room was full and there was a long line of people waiting at the helpdesk. He stood there and tried to calm himself. Being panicked wouldn't do any good. If he'd remembered his badge, he could have gone back into the treatment area, but it was lying on his dresser. He usually worked the late shift when he covered the ER, so he didn't know the clerk at the desk.

"Dr. Fairfield? Are you okay? What are you doing here?"

He turned, relieved to see a face he knew. "Audra, are you on shift?" at her nod he smiled. "A friend of mine was brought in about a hour ago, I need to get to her. I forgot my badge."

She put her hand on his arm. "Give me a minute, I'll find out where she is. What's her name?"

"Bette Watson, car accident."

She motioned him to a spot near the door to the treatment area. "I'll be right back."

He stared at his shoes, noticing he hadn't put on any socks and that he was still wearing the sweatpants he'd put on after his shower. No wonder she'd asked if he was okay. At least he'd remembered to grab a shirt.

Tapping his hand against his leg, he wondered what was taking so long. He wasn't used to being on this side of things. What if it was worse than the nurse had let on in the call? What if... He turned at the sound of his name.

"Follow me," Audra instructed as she swiped her badge over the plate next to the door. "They just brought her back from imaging."

He followed behind her, his stomach roiling with worry. Imaging. There was a chance of...

The screech of the metal rings on the curtain divider interrupted his thought as Audra pulled it back to allow him to enter. He found Bette laying on a gurney, an icepack held to the side of her face, and blood dotting her shirt.

She looked up and saw him standing there. Her eyes filled with tears as she bit at her lip.

"Hey, it's okay." He pulled the chair up to the head of the bed and sat, his hand going to the icepack. Pulling it away from her face he winced at the discoloration and stitches.

"Is it that bad?" she asked, her eyes wide.

He returned the icepack to its place on her face. "No, but it's going to hurt tomorrow."

A nurse stepped into the cubicle. "Time to take off the icepack." She took it from Bette and placed it on the counter. "The doctor will be in in a moment. He's checking your CAT scan right now."

Mark took Bette's hand and frowned at the blood on her fingers.

"Hey, I'm okay," she said as she squeezed his hand. "And you should be happy I got that CAT scan you wanted me to get."

"Please, don't joke about this. When I got that phone call all I could think about was getting to you. I..." He swallowed and started again. "I love you."

"You what?"

He blew out a breath and repeated, "I love you."

"Then why were you avoiding me?"

He ran his hands over his face. "Can we talk about it later? This isn't the place to discuss it."

Tears filled her eyes. "You think I'm crazy." She shrank away from him. "I get it."

His stomach knotted at the anguish on her face. "No, that's not it. Can we please talk about this later? Believe me, we have no privacy here."

101

The curtain was pulled open, and a doctor in scrubs walked in followed by Audra. "Mark, good to see you." He turned his attention to Bette. "I'm Dr. Carson. Good news, the scans are clear. There's no sign of concussion. You'll just need to take it easy for a few days."

Mark picked up Bette's hand and kissed her fingers as he fought back tears.

"When can I get out of here?" Bette asked, a smile on her face.

Audra handed her some papers. "How about now? I've got your discharge instructions right here. I'm sure Mark can explain anything you don't understand."

Bette looked from Audra to Mark. "You know her?"

"Yeah, she's worked a few shifts with me." He looked up at Audra and smiled. "If I hadn't run into her, I'd probably still be trying to get back here to you. The waiting room was packed." Looking back at Bette, he saw her trying to hide a frown. "Hey, what's wrong?"

She sighed. "Nothing. I'm just ready to get out of here."

"Let me go find a wheelchair," Audra commented. With a flick of the curtain, she was out of sight.

Now that the cute nurse was gone, Bette relaxed. "I'm sorry you had to rush over here." She pushed herself up and sat on the side of the bed.

"I'm just glad you're okay. Do you remember what happened?"

"I was on the interstate and had just gotten up to speed when a car swerved into me from two lanes over. My car spun and I hit the guardrail. The next thing I knew, someone was tapping on the window and asking if I was okay."

"You were lucky. A few stitches and a knot on your head, it could have been a lot worse." He pulled out his phone and scrolled to find a number.

"Who are you calling?" she asked as she checked to be sure she had all of her belongings.

"Calling off my shift this afternoon."

"Why? I'm okay, you don't need to …"

He interrupted, "We need to talk and I'm not putting it off. I'll tell them I can be on call but that I need to be with you." He stepped out of the treatment room, phone to his ear.

Bette's mind reeled. He wanted her to go away, to go back to Denver. His explanation that it would stop the episodes while giving her time to hone her magical abilities sounded reasonable, but her heart thought otherwise. It might take her years to become proficient enough to handle the unbinding spell. No way would she agree to be apart from him for that long.

The thoughts whirling in her brain made her headache worse. Leaving felt like giving up. Giving up on her life here and giving up on them. They'd finally found each other, and she wasn't about to let her ancestor tear them apart.

Mark returned with a glass of water and a couple of acetaminophen tablets. "This should help your headache," he said as she held out her hand for the pills.

"Thanks," she mumbled before taking them with a sip of water.

"Just relax, we'll figure this out."

Tears filled her eyes. "You want me to leave."

"Dammit, quit saying it like it's what I want. I don't want you to leave but it might be best."

"It might be, but there's no way to know how long it will take for me to control my magic enough for the spell to work." She angrily wiped at the damned tears running down her cheeks. Stupid headache. "I don't want to leave. My life in Denver was so lonely."

He climbed into the bed and curled his body around hers, as if willing himself to become one with her. "I just..." he started and stopped. "Watching her take over your life is killing me. The headaches last longer each time. What if one day she doesn't leave? Then we really will be apart forever."

"Lisha gave me something to work on to help keep her at bay for a while."

"Seeing you in pain almost every day?" he whispered into her hair, "I don't know how much more I can take."

She rolled over to face him. His haunted eyes watched her as she brushed back the hair at his temple. "Let me try this. Please?" She kissed him. "If it doesn't work, I'll consider leaving for a while."

He pulled her close and snuggled up to her.

Please let this work.

The next morning, Bette handed Mark a to-go mug of coffee and shoved him out of the kitchen. "Go. Sand something or pound some nails because I've got something to work on."

He turned around and kissed her. "Holler if you need me, I won't go far."

She kissed him back. "I know."

Once he was off to do whatever, she walked down the back hallway to the small room where she'd been practicing her magic. It had a large window that let in a lot of natural sunlight. Spreading the mat out in the middle of the room, she sat and put on her meditation music. Lisha had told her it might be possible for her to build a mental wall to keep Lizzie at bay, at least until she figured out a way around it.

Deep breaths helped relax her as she mentally worked on building the wall. Slowly and quietly, she mentally built it brick by mental brick. *There*, she thought as she pushed the last brick into place. *I hope that holds you for a while.*

A tapping on the closed door pulled her out of the self-induced trance. She blinked, noticing how the light from the window had dimmed.

"Bette?"

She shook her head to dispel the last of the trance. "Coming," she shouted as she tried to stand. "Just a sec," she called out at she fell back to the mat, her legs full of pins and needles. *Geez, how long have I been sitting here?* Pain shot through her legs as she hobbled over to the door and unlocked it.

Mark stared at her as she swayed on her feet, falling right into his arms. "Hey, you okay?" he asked worriedly. He picked her up and carried her out to the living room, then set her on the couch. "Let me get you some water."

Leaning back into the cushion, she yawned and closed her eyes.

"Look at me, beautiful," Mark said as he shined a penlight into her eyes. Next came the blood pressure cuff.

"I'm okay. Just stiff from sitting in one position for too long."

He frowned as he took her pulse. "A little fast," he muttered. "And you're breathing is a little fast, too." He dug through his bag for his stethoscope. "How much have you had to drink today?"

She grimaced. "Nothing since the coffee this morning."

"Jesus, you're probably dehydrated." He hurried out of the room and returned with a glass of water. "Drink this. Slowly."

"I'll be okay," she said as she let the water trickle down her dry throat.

"I'll be the judge of that. Another sip," he ordered.

She complied, watching him over the rim of the glass.

"Better?" he asked.

"Yeah," she replied, sipping at the water.

He continued to stare at her.

"What?"

He raised a brow. "Well?"

"Well, what?" she asked, knowing perfectly well what he wanted to know.

"Jesus," he muttered, "such a wiseass." He motioned for her to take another sip. "Did it work?"

"I think so. I don't hear her muttering in my head."

Chapter Eighteen

BETTE SAT on the edge of the bed and stretched before grabbing her phone to check the time. Eleven a.m.? No way. She never slept that late. Stumbling to the bathroom, she found a sticky note on the mirror.

Went into town for some varnish for the floor. Back in a few. Love you. M.

She pulled the note off the mirror and held it to her chest. They had to find a permanent solution to her problem. She couldn't move back to Denver. She'd finally found love and she wasn't going to give it up now. Besides, she just signed the lease on the space for her store, Bette's Beautiful Things would have a home here in Fairfield Corners.

A door banged downstairs as she stepped out of the shower. "Mark? That you?"

After pulling on Mark's robe, she tiptoed down the stairs. The cold from the hardwood floors seeped into her feet, making her shiver. "Mark?" she called as she wandered the first floor.

Another bang came from the back of the house. Returning to the kitchen, she started down the back hallway. The door banged again, and it was definitely the door to her magic room. Marching down the hallway, she turned the knob and opened the door a crack. It slammed in her face and then creaked open.

"Okay, you have my attention." She stepped into the room, pulling the collar of the robe up around her neck to keep out the cold breeze. A slithering sound brought her attention to the table under the window where a book was inching toward the edge, finally falling off onto the floor. The book opened and pages flipped as if being turned by a ghostly hand, finally stopping.

"There's something you want me to see?" *Great, now I'm talking to an empty room.*

She looked down at her feet when a cold draft wound around her ankles. When she looked up, she gasped at the opaque figure standing before her. This must be Mark's great grandfather.

Her knees threatened to buckle under the wave of sadness that rolled through her.

He pointed down at the book.

"Okay, I need to read this. I get it," she said as she bent down to pick up the volume. The spell book they'd found in the trunk was open to the binding spell. "Yes, I know that's what she did. I'm not strong enough to undo the spell yet."

The book trembled in her hands, flipping to the unbinding spell.

"I know. I need to control my magic enough to successfully cast it." Another wave of sadness brought tears to her eyes. "He doesn't blame you." She hoped that was true.

Another tear rolled down her cheek and the ghost reached out to her, swiping at its salty trail. "I don't, either." She shivered at the cold of his finger on her cheek. "I'll do whatever's best for him. If that is me leaving, I'll do it."

The pressure in the room changed, growing as the figure of Mark's grandfather grew more solid. "No!"

The force of that one word blasted through her, the sound of it echoed through the room.

"Bette?" Mark's voice rang out, full of worry.

"I'm okay," she replied, glancing at Mark in the doorway. "I was just having a discussion with your great grandfather."

The figure disappeared with a pop.

"Guess we're done," she muttered as she set the book on the table.

"He showed me the unbinding spell. I think he was telling me that's what we need to do."

Mark stepped closer and pulled her into his arms. "You're shivering. Let's get you warm."

"Coffee first. I was headed down to the kitchen when he showed up."

"My girl wants coffee, she gets coffee," he said into her hair before leading her out of the room.

Chapter Nineteen

KEYS IN HAND, Bette walked up to the front door of what would soon be Bette's Beautiful Things. She slid the key into the lock and squealed when it turned easily. It was really happening. She was going to have a physical store. Stepping into the space, she twirled around and laughed. It was real!

"Bette?"

She stopped twirling and the world tilted for a moment. "Whoopsie, guess I made myself dizzy." She looked over at the new hole in the wall between her store and Cassie's bookstore. The workmen had finished it off with some nice trim and you almost couldn't tell it was new. The freshly sealed hardwood floor gleamed and the walls had been painted.

Cassie had pulled back the plastic sheeting that was the only thing separating the two spaces. "It looks amazing."

"It does. I can't wait for the displays I ordered to arrive tomorrow."

Cassie's footsteps echoed in the empty space. They both turned when the door opened.

Mark waltzed in carrying a long flat box, followed by Logan. "Here, hold this," he said as he handed it to Bette.

"What's going on?" she asked as Mark and Logan went into the storeroom, then returned carrying a wood shelving unit and set it against the back wall behind the counter. "Oooh, it's beautiful."

"After you picked out your displays, I had my guys make this for the wall behind the cash register."

Still holding the box, she leaned over and kissed him. "It's amazing. Thank you."

A corner of the box poked into his arm. "Oh, and this." He took the box out of her hands and laid it on the counter. He opened it and pulled out a placard with the logo she'd designed. "I also had this made to match the big sign outside."

She ran her hands over the metal, amazed at this man. "How did you…?"

"I had to be sneaky. I wanted it to be a surprise," he took her hand and kissed her knuckles, "but I know someone who works at the shop where you had the sign outside made. He helped me out."

"That you would think to do this…" she kissed him again. "Now I really can't wait for the displays to arrive."

She hadn't noticed Cassie slipping away until she reappeared with a bottle of champagne and some plastic glasses. "I was going to save this for your grand opening, but I think we should open this now."

Logan took the bottle and opened it with a pop, pouring the bubbly liquid into the four glasses. "To Bette's Beautiful Things. May it be all that you imagined."

Dressed in jeans and a sweater, she watched the shadows lengthening in the fields as they drove down the country road. The impromptu celebration in the new store had been amazing, but now Mark was taking her to the infamous island, a peninsula on the shore of Little Beaver Lake. Fall weather had arrived and she was slightly worried about it being too cold. *Maybe we should have brought heavier coats.*

"What's going on in that brain of yours?" Mark asked as he turned onto the road that led to the lake. "You're worried about something, I can tell."

"Isn't it kinda chilly to be by the lake after dark? Won't we be cold?"

"Don't worry, I've got you covered," he said with a laugh. "I would never plan something that…"

"Oh, I didn't mean anything by it. Just my brain focusing on something inconsequential."

He took her hand into his. "Okay, duly noted. Your brain fixates on things. Got it."

She shrugged. "I know it's silly, but I just can't help it."

Mark pulled into the meadow and parked the truck. "Grab the blankets and stuff out of the back of the truck, I'll get the cooler."

Her arms full of blankets, she trotted after him toward the lake, trying to watch her footing in the growing darkness.

The ground under her feet changed from dirt to sand. When she looked up, Bette saw the lake spread out before her, the lights from the few cottages on the shore shined like beacons in the darkness. "Oooh, it's beautiful."

Mark set the cooler down near the fire pit. "Spread the blanket out over here and I'll build us a fire."

Before long, Mark had a blaze going. He sat on the blanket next to Bette and pulled her into his arms. He pointed across the lake, "See those lights? That's Robbie and Faith's place. They're the only ones who live on the lake year 'round. The rest are summer cottages."

She snuggled closer. "Can they see us?"

"No, not really. Not unless they have binoculars."

"They could be watching us?"

He laughed. "I'm sure Robbie and Faith have better things to do than watch us over here."

"See, I told you my brain focuses on weird stuff." She shivered.

"Cold? I've got something that will help with that." He squeezed her hand and then got up and pulled a thermos out of the bag along with a couple of disposable cups. Filling both, he handed her one. "Hot chocolate with a shot of Irish Crème."

"Yum," she said after she took a sip. "This is nice."

He unfolded the other blanket and wrapped it around their shoulders. "Better?"

"Much. Now, what's in the cooler?"

He looked away and said, "Sandwiches and potato salad for when we get hungry.

"What are you hiding in there?"

Feigning innocence, he replied, "Nothing."

"Yeah, right. You're awful at keeping secrets."

"Well, I had this whole thing planned out, but I guess it's kinda cheesy. In high school, this was the place to celebrate anything big. Birthdays, anniversaries, asking someone to go steady, graduation. You get the idea."

"Mark Fairfield, are you asking me to go steady?"

"Not exactly." He dug his hand into his jacket pocket and pulled out a small velvet box.

"What is this?"

"I know it's soon, and with everything going on it might be the wrong thing to do, but..." He flipped open the box and showed her the solitaire diamond ring nestled there. "I can't imagine my life without you."

She stared at the ring, her emotions warring with her head. "But what if..."

"No buts or what ifs allowed. Even if, *especially* if, we have to be apart for a while. I want us to be connected. To make this commitment to each other."

His phone rang. "This better not be the hospital," he muttered.

"Yeah," he answered gruffly. He listened and then replied, "No, not yet." Another pause. "Okay, okay. Hang on."

Turning to Bette he handed her his phone. "It's Robbie and Faith. They want to know your answer."

"Oh my God, they can definitely see us!" She took the phone from his hand. "Hey guys, what do you think? Should I say yes?"

She nodded. "Okay." Disconnecting the call, she handed the phone back. "Here you go."

"So?"

"Huh?"

"So, what's your answer?"

"Let me think…"

Mark grabbed her and pulled her down onto the blanket. "Quit toying with me. What's your answer?"

"Well," she started, and he snorted.

"Quit stalling."

"Okay, fine," she sighed. "Yes."

He slipped the ring on her finger and stared at it before rolling her onto her back. Covering her body with his, he kissed her.

She was enjoying the feel of Mark's body against hers, the feel of his lips on hers, the feel of his hands in her hair. Then she heard someone clear their throat.

Mark's warmth left her and she sat up, brushing her hair out of her eyes.

"I've been standing here for five minutes. Did you bother to let her come up for air?" Robbie asked with a grin.

"Oh, so you like to watch? Watch this?" Mark said before grabbing her and kissing her again.

She slapped Mark's shoulder. "Stop it, you two. Seriously."

"Sorry, Bette, but these two can be a bit…immature," Faith commented.

Bette put her arms around Mark's waist and pulled him close, reaching up to kiss him. "Good to know."

"So, Cassie has a big mouth." Mark commented as he pulled out two more cups and poured hot chocolate for Robbie and Faith.

"Actually, it was Adam, so everyone probably knows by now."

Robbie took a sip and took the cup out of Faith's hand. "That's got alcohol in it."

Mark looked at Robbie and then at Faith. "You're…"

"Yep," Robbie crowed. "Just found out for sure today."

"Now we have even more reason to celebrate."

They all turned when another vehicle pulled into the meadow. Slamming doors heralded the arrival of Ragan, Adam, Cassie, and Logan.

"This is turning into a regular party," Mark grumbled.

"So, what's the other reason we're celebrating?" Cassie asked.

Ragan grinned.

"You already know, don't you?" Faith asked. "Impossible to have a secret around here for more than five minutes. I'll just confirm it." Robbie pulled her close and kissed her. "We're pregnant!"

The women squealed and the guys went to the vehicles and grabbed some chairs.

Mark and Bette watched from their seats on the blanket, amazed at how their friends had horned in on their private celebration. No matter what the future brought, they'd have this moment out here on the beach with their friends.

Chapter Twenty

As the workmen placed the displays, Bette stared at the ring on her left hand. She hoped accepting his proposal was the right thing to do. There were so many things that could go wrong. A week ago she was sure he was going to end things, and now they were engaged.

"I remember that feeling," Ragan commented as she walked across the store.

"What?"

"That feeling like it's not quite real so you sneak a glance at the ring to verify that it really did happen." Ragan handed a cup of coffee to Bette. "I figured you could use this. I'm sure you had a hard time falling asleep last night."

"Actually, no. Once I curled up in Mark's arms, I was out like a light." She sipped at the coffee, sighing as the caffeine hit her system. "What brings you to town today?"

"I wanted to get Jordan a thank you gift for watching all the kids last night. I know you've got something that's perfect. You always do."

"About that... How did you know Mark was going to pop the question last night?" She watched Ragan's cheeks flush.

"Well, I had a vision, and I knew it was going to go down when Mark mentioned he was taking you out to The Island yesterday. We waited just down the road from The Island until Robbie called us."

"So that's how you all got there so fast," Bette replied before taking another sip of coffee.

"We were all so excited for the two of you. I knew Mark would find someone perfect for him."

"Your visions have been busy this week between Mark's proposal and Robbie and Faith being pregnant again."

"Sometimes it's really hard to keep things secret."

"I bet. Now, what did you have in mind for Jordan? I'm not officially open yet but I've got most of my stock here. I'm waiting for the workmen to finish setting up the displays before stocking the shelves."

She was wrapping Ragan's purchase in tissue paper when Faith peeked in around the plastic sheeting. "Oh good, you're here."

"I hope I have this much foot traffic when I'm actually open," Bette mumbled as she slipped the wrapped item into a bag emblazoned with the name of her shop. "Here you go, Ragan. I hope Jordan likes it."

"I'm sure she will," Ragan replied as she walked over to the plastic sheeting. She caught Faith's attention and nodded slightly before slipping out of the space into the bookstore.

Bette stared at her contemplatively. Something was up, but she didn't know what.

"I need a gift for my agent. It's her birthday next week and I…"

"And you need it right away, right?"

"Yes, I've been putting off buying something, I've been so busy getting this story written that I haven't had time to pick something out."

Bette supposed that could be true. Maybe she was making more of a thing that her two friends stopped by than it was.

"You mentioned before she loves flowers. Hmm… I think I've got just the thing." She motioned to the chair behind the counter when she noticed Faith looked a little green. "Why don't you sit down? You want some water or something?"

Faith swallowed hard. "No, it's fine. It'll pass in a minute."

As she watched, Faith's color returned to normal. "Well, you look better now but I'd feel more comfortable if you'd sit for a minute." Once her friend was seated, she handed her the clear acrylic block with a single perfect daisy embedded in the middle of it. "I know it's kitschy, but I think she'd love it."

"It's perfect. I'll send it to her along with a bouquet of daisies and a silly card."

Once Bette had it packaged and bagged, she handed the bag to Faith. "You still look a little green. Go home and relax a bit before you get back to writing."

"I will," Faith replied as she hugged Bette. "So much good news lately." With a wave, her friend was out the door.

No more than five minutes passed before Cassie wandered over from the bookstore. "I wanted to see the displays," she shrugged at Bette's pointed look.

"You're the third one of my friends to stop by this morning. Mark put you up to this, didn't he?"

Cassie's cheeks pinked. "Were we that obvious? You know he's just worried about you. I don't blame him, having witnessed Lizzie for myself."

Bette sank down into the chair. "I don't blame him either, but he needs to chill out about it a bit."

"How is the wall holding up? Your mood seems better since the day you put it up."

Bette stared at her hands in her lap. "Well, to be honest it's not perfect."

"Has Lizzie been causing you trouble again?"

"No, but I can hear her in my head. It's just a whisper, but I'm afraid she'll figure out how to tear down the wall and I'll lose myself for good." She wiped at a stray tear. "Dammit, I'm not going to let her ruin my life."

Cassie whipped out her phone. "You need to—"

Bette stood and put her hand on Cassie's arm. "Don't you dare call Mark. He's worried enough as it is. He thinks he's hiding it, but I can see it in his eyes."

"Only if you promise you'll tell him if it gets worse."

Bette rolled her eyes. "I suppose."

"Not good enough. Promise me or I'm calling him right now."

"Okay, okay. I promise."

Two hours later she stood at Lisha's door, willing her hand to press the doorbell when the door opened.

"You coming in or what? I've been waiting for you to ring the bell for ten minutes."

"Sorry, I guess the whole controlling my power thing scares me more than I want to admit."

Lisha led her down the hall to the den where they'd practiced several times. "Come in and relax. I'll make some tea and we'll get you prepped for a productive session." She whirled around, her dress flaring out and her scarf trailing behind her. "Sit tight, I'll be right back."

Bette pulled her journal out of her purse and turned to the page where she'd written the instructions for the fire summoning spell. According to Lisha, creating and controlling fire was the best way to learn to control the power within her, the power she'd just recently learned she possessed. She read through the incantation a couple of times and closed her eyes, committing the words to memory.

Taking a cleansing breath, she practiced the preparation techniques Lisha taught her during her last visit. Concentrating on her breathing, she cleared her mind and focused on finding her serenity. Until Lizzie's voice rose slightly.

Is she getting through the wall? What could she do if she managed to break down my mental wall?

"Bette? Are you okay?" Lisha peered into her eyes. "Tell me what's going on."

She forced herself to take a deep breath and try to get her thoughts in order. "Well, I'm scared. I can hear Lizzie's voice, and it seems to be getting louder."

Lisha took Bette's hands and squeezed them. "Don't worry, we'll shore up that wall and keep her out until we're ready to deal with her. Now, relax and do your breathing exercises while I poke around and check out this mental wall you've built."

Bette's fingertips tingled as Lisha's power flowed through her, the warm rush comforting in a way. Focused on keeping her breaths deep and even, she didn't notice when Lisha dropped her hands. The extra oomph Lisha had used on the wall had silenced Lizzie's voice, at least for the time being.

"Bette?"

Bette blinked, raising herself out of the self-induced trancelike state she'd been in.

"Ooooh, that's much better. I can't hear her at all, now."

"Good. I didn't have to do much. Your wall was sturdy, it just needed a nudge." She poured them both a cup of tea and poured in plenty of sugar. "Drink this, and then you can practice controlling the fire spell."

A week later, she saw Mark watching out the window as she sped up the driveway and screeched to a halt next to his car. He was wearing his worried face. God, why couldn't she keep to a schedule?

She ran up the porch steps and opened the door with one hand while her other was rummaging in her purse for her cell phone. "I'm sorry I'm late. My phone died and I couldn't find my cord, and…" She made an oof sound when she ran into him.

His arms went around her and pulled her in for a hug. She dropped everything she was carrying to hug him back. "It's okay. I was worried but I'll get over it." She looked up into his eyes and he smiled. "Hi, beautiful."

"Hi, handsome. I got to Lisha's late and then I had to run home to pick up the bag I forgot this morning. I'm just a hot mess today."

"I know how we can fix that."

"Fix what?"

"Make it so you don't have to remember to bring an overnight bag with you." He kissed her and then picked up her stuff with one hand, the other grabbing hers and pulling her down the hall into the kitchen. "You could move in here with me. I mean, we are engaged."

She stopped, watching as he set her bag on the stairs and then continued on into the kitchen. She hitched herself up onto a bar stool and silently watched him pour some oil into the wok and turn on the burner. "You're serious, aren't you?"

Transferring a container from the fridge to the counter, he turned and looked at her. "Why wouldn't I be? I love you, and I've gotten used to you being in my bed." He looked at her and arched a brow. "I thought this is something you'd want."

"Oh, it is. I'm just surprised. We haven't even talked about moving in together."

"Every time I bring it up, you change the subject." After a long look at her, he turned back to the stove and transferred chunks of chicken to the wok to cook. The empty container went in the dishwasher, then he washed his hands before turning back to her.

She loved watching him cook. It wasn't her thing, though she did love to bake. "It was just a couple of weeks ago you were pushing me away. Give a girl a minute to catch up."

He turned her on the stool so she was facing him. "Can we quit rehashing that? At the time, I thought that was the only way we could keep you safe. Seeing you turn into Lizzie scares me more every time it happens. I'm sorry I didn't handle it well." He leaned in and kissed her. "I love you so much I was willing to send you away because I thought it was best for you. Pushing you away hurt more than you can imagine."

She put her hands on either side of his face and peered into his eyes. "I get why you did it, and I love you all the more for it. And yes, I'll move in here with you as long as my mental wall keeps Lizzie at bay. If it starts to crumble, I'll go back to my house in Fort Wayne. I can't take the chance of her hurting you."

He put his forehead against hers and sighed.

A burning smell wafted over them. "What's burning?"

"Oh shit! The chicken!" He hurried over to the stove, pulled off the smoking pan, and put it in the sink. "See what you do to me? I can't even make a simple stir fry when you're around."

With a giggle, she slid off the barstool as he opened the freezer. "Do you have some ground beef? I can make nachos if you do."

"You know, this will only be the second time you've cooked for me. We always seem to order pizza when we're at your place."

"Well, when you have the best pizza place in Fort Wayne close to your house…"

"True." He turned to her, a package of frozen hamburger in his hand. "Let me start getting this defrosted, then I'll shred some cheese."

"Sounds like a plan," she replied as she searched through his cupboards for the butcher block.

"What are you looking for?"

"I need a cutting board and a knife. I know you have tomatoes and onion, and they'll be good on the nachos."

When he bent over and pulled the butcher block from the lower cabinet next to the stove, she eyed his butt. "I think I'm going to like this living together thing," she muttered before turning to the fridge to grab the tomatoes and onion.

After she'd chopped the tomatoes, she started in on the onion, brushing at a stray tear.

"Hey, what's wrong?" she heard Mark say just before he put his hand on her shoulder and turned her to face him.

"Nothing, it's just the onions."

"I thought maybe you'd changed your mind about moving in."

She set the knife on the counter and wiped her hands on the damp dish rag before clasping them behind Mark's neck. "I promise I won't change my mind."

"I know that deep down, but part of me is still worried that the Fairfield curse will strike and I'll be left here alone." He kissed her lightly and then set her back from him. "I don't think I'd survive that. Now, get back to those onions, woman."

Picking up the knife, she smiled sadly at how her ancestor had cursed his family. Would they have found each other without Lizzie's influence? She still wondered if Lizzie had been behind Dane's father kidnapping her and bringing her here. What if they hadn't had that built-in connection?

She forced her attention to the knife in her hand just before it seemed to move on its own and slice into her finger. "Dammit!" she yelled as she dropped the knife and reached for the dish rag.

Mark grabbed her hand and pulled her over to the sink. Turning on the faucet, he held her fingers still while water ran over the cut.

"Shit, that stings," she muttered as he pulled her hand out of the stream of water and inspected the cut. "It doesn't look too bad, probably doesn't need stitches."

She watched a fat drop of blood splash into the sink and mix with the water droplets, turning them pink. Swallowing hard, her mind started to float away.

Mark pulled her against him when her knees buckled. "Hang on Bette. Don't pass out on me."

She tried to focus on his voice, but all she could think about was her blood dripping out of her finger into the sink. The world went gray.

"Bette?"

Blinking, she looked up into Mark's eyes. "What happened?" she mumbled. "Why am I lying on the floor?"

With a smile Mark replied, "I didn't want to get blood on the sofa."

"Oh, right. I cut my finger."

"How can someone who loves bloody slasher movies get woozy at the sight of a little blood?"

"Yeah, well, it's different when it's your own blood."

He helped her sit up and lean against the cupboard. "Just sit there a minute while I get the first aid kit from the pantry." She avoided looking at her hand other than taking a quick glance to see a dish towel wrapped around her finger.

Kit in hand, he dropped down next to her and unwrapped the towel, smiling at her grimace. "This will sting," he warned her before spraying disinfectant on the cut.

Studiously staring at the ceiling to avoid looking at her finger, she grimaced at the pain.

"It's not too deep, so it won't need any stitches." He rummaged in the kit and pulled out gauze and tape. "I'll get that fixed up and then finish chopping the onions. No more knives for my girl."

She smiled at the love she heard in his voice. And then she remembered how the knife had seemed to move on its own to cut her finger. "Uh, as soon as you're done patching me up, I think I better call Lisha."

"Why? What's wrong?"

"The knife moved on its own, and I can feel Lizzie's magic seeping through some cracks in my mental wall."

With a frown, Mark finished up and closed the first aid kit. "You sit there and I'll get you a glass of water." Filling a tumbler and placing it in front of her, he pulled out his phone. "I'll call Lisha and talk to her first."

"You don't trust me to tell you what she says?"

"It's not that."

Chapter Twenty-One

BETTE'S HANDS trembled as she gathered the ingredients for the spell and arranged them on the kitchen table. "Think of it as a recipe you're cooking," she muttered to herself. Making sure she'd collected everything, Bette placed all the items in her favorite tote bag. The mental wall she'd built to keep Elizabeth locked away was crumbling fast, so they couldn't put off casting the spell any longer. The itch in her subconscious grew as her ancestor battered at the mental barrier. Her grasp of witchcraft was shaky at best, so the coven would be performing the actual spell. However, Lisha had pointed out that her gathering the ingredients would help make the spell stronger.

The alarm on her phone went off, reminding her it was time to prepare herself for the ritual. Soon, Mark would be there to pick her up. Placing the bag near the door, she sat in her favorite chair and scrolled through the music on her phone, selecting the mystical soundtrack she'd downloaded the day before. Soothing tones washed over her as she closed her eyes and focused on her breathing. The music swelled around her as she concentrated, swirling shapes of color filling her mind.

A soft knock brought her attention back to her surroundings. Pleased with her progress, she glanced at her phone and saw it was time to meet the coven. She was surprised to find Cassie and Ragan standing outside her door, with Faith waiting in the car. "What are you three doing here?"

"Lisha called and asked us to pick you up."

"Mark was supposed to come get me..."

Cassie interrupted her, "Lisha wanted to talk to him alone before you arrive." She picked up the tote bag. "Got everything?"

"I think so," Bette replied, her brow drawn with worry. "What if this doesn't work?"

"Don't talk like that," Ragan said as she snuffed out the candles Bette had lit as part of her preparation. "Let's do this."

The sun warmed the side of her face through the window of Cassie's car. She'd taken the beautiful fall weather as a good omen, needing something to help her face the afternoon and the spellwork that would be needed. Casting out a previous incarnation wasn't easy, but it was possible if Lisha's coven was right.

She was surprised when Cassie stopped and parked. They were at Mark's house instead of the clearing out in the woods she'd assumed they'd use for the ritual.

"Lisha called and changed the location after talking with Mark yesterday. Lizzie is closely linked to Mark's great grandfather, and he's strongest in Mark's ancestral home."

"That makes sense," she mumbled, wishing the day was already over. She shuffled into the house, breaking into a run and jumping into Mark's arms when she spied him in the hall. Standing on tiptoe, she wrapped her arms around his neck and kissed him, pouring all her love into the caress. Her heart thumped along with his when she dropped her head. She was terrified of what the afternoon might bring.

"What was that for?" he whispered into her hair, only loud enough for her to hear.

"Just in case things don't go as planned today," she admitted.

"Hey, we're going to get through this," he murmured, hugging her tighter. "I'm not losing you now."

"Bette, we're ready to get started," Lisha said from the parlor.

Lacing his fingers through hers, Mark led her into the parlor, giving her hand a squeeze before moving to the position Lisha indicated.

Bette looked at the group from her place in the center of the room. She was surrounded by the twelve witches of Lisha's coven, her friends, and most importantly, Mark. Wiping her hands on her jeans, she sat and tried to clear her mind.

The chanting around her grew louder as the room darkened. The sun suddenly blocked by low, black clouds that rolled in as soon as they'd linked hands around her.

The chanting changed as her mind turned inward, rushing through a dark corridor toward the mental barrier she'd erected against Lizzie. She watched as bricks wiggled out and fell away until the wall crumbled into a pile at her feet.

Vaguely aware of the strobe-like effect of the lightning out in the physical world, she approached Lizzie and held out her hand.

With a laugh Lizzie swept past her, "I hope you said goodbye." And the wall was back, locking her into the recesses of her mind. Raising her arms, she pounded on the wall and yelled for Mark—for anyone—to help her.

Lizzie opened her eyes and zeroed in on Mark and the hazy apparition standing behind him. "My soldier," she whispered as the form floated toward her.

Reaching up to her face, she felt his hand brush at her cheek. The crackle of energy zipped through her.

The chanting changed and the words pulled at her, trying to pull her from Bette's body.

Marcus held out his hand, "You don't belong here."

Snapping herself out of the trance induced by the chanting, she glared at the Union soldier standing in front of her, resplendent in his officer uniform. "You left," she screamed as energy whipped through her, her hair standing on end as thunder boomed. "You left me to be married off to an awful man. My father told me you left without fighting for me." Eyes glowing and hair whipping around her, she raised her hands and gathered her power, preparing to hurl it at the offending figure.

Unaffected by her show of power, Marcus stood tall. "I had no choice."

"You left me!" she screamed and hurled a ball of energy at him.

He stepped aside and brought his hands up to grab her arms. "I planned to come back later and spirit you away, but your father had me arrested. It took me three days to clear my name. By the time I was able to get back to your father's house, you were gone. Married to someone else and on your way to another state."

She flinched at the anguish in his voice. "But you forgot about me."

"I didn't forget. Sure, I came home and found love again, but I never forgot you—my first love, my Lizzie." He reached into his pocket and pulled out a small frame, turning it to show her the picture lovingly placed inside. "I carried this in my pocket every day in life, and now in death." He gripped the frame tighter as he stared at her. "You need to release them and come with me. Release the curse and let my family be." He held out his hand toward her. "Please, my love. Find your peace."

The chanting changed again. Their words pulled at her, wrenching her away from Bette's body. "I'm not ready," she screamed. She raised her arms and pushed magical energy out in a circle around her.

The unearthly shockwave threatened to break their physical connection. Hands grasped tightly, the coven chanted louder, pushing their own magic up as a barrier, and then stepping back as they were pummeled by the burst.

With a loud pop, Lizzie's connection with Bette's body was severed and Bette dropped to the ground as Lizzie was hurled toward Mark.

Watching Bette, Mark was surprised when Lizzie swept through him, the force of her energy knocking him on his ass.

Unbound from Bette's body, Lizzie worked to stop herself in front of Marcus, finally able to materialize as a semi-solid form.

The spell complete, the witches stepped back and watched.

Pulling her closer, Marcus sighed as she settled into him. "I've waited so long for this," he murmured to her.

His love washed through her, draining away the hurt, and the hate. "Oh, Marcus," she whispered as she leaned closer, kissing him. With a sad smile, she waved her hand in the air and murmured the words to break the curse that had plagued the Fairfield men. "I'm sorry," she said as the pair faded into nothing.

The wind stopped and the clouds rolled away, letting the sun's rays shine into the room.

Mark sat up and looked at Bette, lying lifeless in the center of the circle.

"No, no, no, no," he whispered as he crawled to her. With a shaky hand, he brushed her hair off her forehead. His body remembered his training, and he checked for a pulse. Pain washed over him, stilling the breath in his lungs. "No!" he screamed as he began CPR, chanting her name under his breath as he worked. "Call 9-1-1," he shouted to Cassie who already had her phone out.

Bette could feel Mark's torment. He was so close, but the wall was in the way. She pulled at the bricks, her consciousness trying to float away. She concentrated on Mark's voice, his anguish called to her. His presence pulled her toward him as the white light behind her awakened her consciousness. The ring Mark placed on her finger a week before began to warm. It held a special kind of magic, the magic of true love. Coursing through her and out her fingertips, Mark's love battered at the mental wall until it burst apart as if blown apart by dynamite. The force of the blast blew her backward toward the blackness of the unknown, while the magic of love pulled her forward toward the physical world. There was blinding pain and then, finally, peace.

She opened her eyes to find Mark hovering over her. At her gasp, his hands stilled from their ministrations. "Bette?" he asked, his voice almost soundless.

"Hey," she replied, bringing her hand up to his face to brush at the tears running down his cheek.

He pulled her close, tucking her head under his chin as he held her. "I thought I'd lost you. You weren't..." he choked as his arms tightened around her.

"It's okay. You pulled me back. Without you, I would have been lost."

Silently, the coven retreated from the room, their presence no longer required. Cassie herded them toward the kitchen. "I think we all need a drink after that." She pulled a bottle of whiskey from the cupboard and took a healthy swig before passing it around. She watched each witch take a sip.

"Is it always this…intense?" she asked.

"No, not usually," Lisha replied after taking a long pull from the bottle. "Lizzie was stronger than I realized."

Bette tucked close to his side, Mark walked into the room and grabbed the bottle of whiskey. After taking a long pull he returned it to the counter. He kissed Bette on top of her head and let her go, pushing her toward Cassie. "Take her upstairs." He turned and faced Lisha, crooking a finger. "You, I need to talk to you," he said, his jaw hard.

Lisha nodded and followed him out of the room as Bette and Cassie went up the staircase.

"What was that about?" Cassie asked as they walked into Mark's bedroom.

Bette held her hand in front of her mouth as she yawned. "Oh geez, that wore me out." She plopped onto the bed and let herself drop back onto the pillows. "It's so quiet in my head now," she murmured as her eyes drifted shut.

Mark propped himself on an elbow and watched her breathe, his chest rising and falling in sync with hers. The ache in his chest had started when she walked into his house the day before, her hair covering the angry, red scar on her forehead. His thoughts had turned somber. He'd almost turned his back on her, but then she'd run toward him and into his arms. It had become impossible to turn off the rush of emotion, the love that coursed through him, no matter what he'd promised himself. His arms wrapped around her had never felt so right. And then that kiss, the kiss that could have been their last.

His heart thumped as his imagination spun out of control, showing him what could have happened. Jumping off the bed, he paced the length of the room as he ran his hands through his hair. By sheer force of will, he kept himself from getting sick. The mere thought of what could have happened made him nauseous. Heat ran through his veins as if trying to burn out his morbid thoughts, sweat drenching his shirt at the armpits and across his back. Forcing air into his lungs, he yanked on the window, straining his biceps when it wouldn't budge. With a shaking hand he flipped the lock and then pushed the window up, breathing deeply as the breeze wafted across his over-heated skin.

"She's okay," he whispered, watching her sleep. Then his imagination started playing horrific scenarios, forcing him to examine the thoughts he'd tamped down. *What if her feelings for me were because of Lizzie? What if Bette doesn't love me?*

Forcing himself to relax, he returned to the bed. Lying down next to her, he draped his arm over her waist and snuggled into her, content to hold her close for as long as she'd let him.

Bette snuggled into the warmth beside her. Blessed quiet. Her eyes popped open at the soft snore in her ear. Carefully, she turned her head to find Mark asleep, his arm draped over her and holding her close. Safe and warm. Best of all, she was finally alone in her head. Sighing, she drifted back to sleep.

She snuggled into the pillow, brushing her fingers at the whisper-soft touches on her ear. "What?" she asked groggily as the touches continued.

"Hey, sleepyhead," Mark said. Propped on his elbow he stared down at her. "You hungry?"

"Mphhhh," she replied, her face in her pillow. The scent of coffee tickled her nose and she opened one eye to look at him, her eyes focusing on the mug in his hand. "That for me?"

"Of course," he said with a grin. "You think I'd wake you without coffee?" He brushed her hair off her forehead and placed a kiss there, watching as she sipped at the coffee, her eyes closed.

"Yes," she said between sips.

"Yes, what?"

"I'm hungry. Starved, actually." Her stomach rumbled as if she hadn't eaten in days. "What time is it?"

"Almost six."

"No wonder I'm still tired, I've only slept three hours."

He burst out laughing.

She narrowed her eyes. "What's so funny?"

"Try about twenty-seven hours. It's six on Wednesday."

She swallowed wrong and choked on her coffee. "What?"

He stuck a thermometer in her mouth and grabbed her wrist to count her pulse. At the beep he removed it and peered at the display. "Normal."

"Stop being all Doctor Fairfield. I'm fine. The paramedics checked me over yesterday."

"Just let me…"

"Seriously," she interrupted him. "I'm fine."

"Who's the doctor here?" he asked with a frown. "You do realize you weren't breathing yesterday, right?"

"Well, yeah, but…"

"But what? Let me do this, so I'll feel better about it." He pushed his medical bag down the bed and sat next to her. "I thought I'd lost you, that it was my turn for the curse to strike." He turned away from her, his hands fisted in his lap.

"Hey, I'm okay."

He stood and stared down at her. "You. Were. *Dead*." He ran his hands through his hair, making it stand up in spikes. "All I could see was living my life without you in it." He turned away and said, "If I'd had a gun in my hand, I would have used it on myself."

She jumped out of bed and wrapped her arms around him from the back. "I'm okay and Lizzie is gone. It's over."

His head bowed as his breath hitched. "But, what if…" he started.

"What if what?"

"What if what you felt for me was Lizzie? Your feelings were so wrapped up in her hate. What if *you* don't have any feelings for *me*?" he asked.

"Look at me," she said, pulling on his arm to turn him to face her.

"I don't want to see the indifference in your eyes."

"Seriously? Mark Fairfield, turn around and LOOK. AT. ME." She waited as he turned and searched her face. "This is me. *Only* me. Believe me, these feelings I have for you? They're real. So real, they scare me."

"Thank God," he said and kissed her, desperate and hungry. "Marry me before you change your mind," he murmured against her lips.

She broke the kiss and looked up at him. "Didn't we already do this? You remember that night out by the lake?"

"Well, yeah, but I mean marry me tomorrow. We'll go down to the courthouse and make it official. After almost losing you, I feel like I need to do this as soon as possible."

She smiled at him. "Of course, I'll marry you whenever you want. I told you, I don't need a big wedding." Picking up her phone she scrolled through her contacts.

"What are you doing?"

"Calling the dress shop next to the bookstore. I saw the perfect dress the other day. I was going to go buy it but I haven't had time, what with getting Lizzie cast out and all."

Mark waited as she talked to the owner of the dress shop, making sure the dress would be ready for her first thing in the morning.

"Now, Doctor Fairfield, that's taken care of." She pulled him close and kissed him. "I'm all set for tomorrow."

He pulled her down so they were laying on the bed. Drawing circles with his finger on her shoulder, he kissed her and pulled the covers up. "Go back to sleep. Tomorrow will be a big day."

Also by L.A. Remenicky

Next Up In The Fairfield Corners Series
Violet Serenade, Book 5
https://books2read.com/Violet-Serenade

Violet Miller has always known she was different. Her very first memories were full of swirling colors instead of music, and then having to suppress the knowledge. Only her family could be trusted with her secret - until the day he arrived.

From the moment Dane McWilliams set eyes on Vi, he knew she was special. Scared, alone, and only seven years old, he lost himself in her deep blue eyes and finally knew safety. For eleven years she was his heart, his home, and on the day he left for basic training he started counting the days until he could return to her.

And then his letters went unanswered

It's been seven years since Vi last set eyes on Dane. Seven years of avoidance and heartache. She no longer the girl he left behind - she's all grown up and has returned to Fairfield Corners with a fiancé in tow. Resigned to a lackluster friendship, Dane's hopes and dreams are shattered. But when an ancient evil returns to wreck havoc on their lives, the truth of Vi's ability is revealed, and with it, the realization that her powers are not the thing she's kept hidden from Dane.

About the Author

Romance author, dialysis warrior, furkid mom, and Best Fiends addict. Lover of coffee, 80's music, and all things romance. During the day she carves out writing time in between trips to the back door as doorman to her four-legged furry child. At night after spending quality time with her husband she chips away at her never-ending TBR pile.

Keep up with Hoosiergirl Publishing here:
https://hoosiergirl-publishing.kit.com/df28902ff9

You can find all her links on her website:
https://www.laremenicky.com

Also from the Lavish Publishing Family

Rendered (Irrevocable Series Book 1)
Samantha Jacobey
https://books2read.com/Rendered

THE END of the world is coming, or so they say, and that puts Bailey Dewitt on a crash course with Armageddon. Orphaned, she and her young brothers find themselves living with their renegade uncle as part of a group of survivalists. She struggles against them, searching for a way to escape, but every discovery only terrifies her more.

For Caleb Cross, the Ranch is a way of life. The members of their group are family, and none should come between them. Smitten from the moment he met Bailey, his choices are no longer easy, his path no longer clear. He wants to welcome her and the twins into their fold and hopes his kin will agree.

. . .

But the elders who lead them aren't interested in the troublesome girl. They are plotting for the time they will be rid of her and expect Caleb to go along with their plans - he is after all one of them.

At first, Bailey resists Caleb's charms, but soon must admit that she desperately needs a friend. She has no intention of anything more, but when the elders make their move, she is forced to trust him with her very life.

They both have hard lessons to learn. Relationships built on secrets and lies don't come with guarantees. When the world falls apart around them, some things are Irrevocable.

Realistic sci-fi and romantic suspense will pull you into to the first book of the Irrevocable Trilogy.

Summer's Deceit (The Trilogy Book 1)
Sara J. Bernhardt
https://books2read.com/SummersDeceit

Jane Callahan is a reclusive, seventeen-year-old high school student dealing with the death of her beloved brother. Her home in Southern California with her mother is a constant reminder of her loss and pain. In hopes of escaping her past she moves to North Bend Oregon to live with her father, where she meets a beautiful boy named Aidan Summers.

Jane is intrigued by his looks as well as his unusual ways of attempting to get her attention. After months of uncommon conversation and frustration, an uncertain romance brews between Jane and Aidan, but Aidan has a ghastly secret that could destroy everything.

Get swept away by The Hunter's Trilogy – YA romantic suspense with a paranormal twist.

Midnight Owl: Joe Leverette Mysteries, Book 1
https://www.lavishpublishing.com/authors/viv-drewa/

Can a sensitive and an owl help the police find a horrible murderer.

www.ingramcontent.com/pod-product-compliance
Lightning Source LLC
Chambersburg PA
CBHW072027170626
46811CB00008B/2977